Published by Steve Guettermann

This is a work of fiction. Names, characters and events are products of the author's imagination, or are used fictitiously, and are not to be construed as real. Any resemblance to actual events, organizations or persons, living or dead, is entirely coincidental.

Comments? Questions? Email the author at: migratoryanimal@gmail.com. or JuliusV@juliusvwarriorpope.com. Please try to remember to put Julius V in the subject line. More author and book information is available at www.juliusVwarriorpope.com and https://www.facebook.com/JuliusV.WarriorPope

If you wish to receive advance notice as to when the sequel is available, please email migratoryanimal@gmail.com or JuliusV@juliusvwarriorpope.com. And again, try to remember to put Julius V in the subject line.

ISBN-13: 978-0-9860939-0-6
ISBN-10: 0986093904

Reviews

Here's what a few people might say about *Julius V~Warrior Pope* if they were alive today.

~

"*Julius V~Warrior Pope,* now THAT is a divine comedy!"
Dante Alighieri – Author of The Divine Comedy
~

"The most accurate portrayal of convent life I've ever read!"
Mother Theresa – aka The Cutie of Calcutta
~

"The BEST archetypal humor I've ever read!"
Carl Jung – Psychologist and author of *The Archetypes and The Collective Unconscious*
~

"*Julius V~Warrior Pope* is music to my ears!"
Ludwig von Beethoven – Famous composer
~

"We could have used Sister LaTrelle against the English."
Joan of Arc – Catholic Saint
~

"After reading *Julius V~Warrior Pope*, my hero now has a thousand and one faces!"
Joseph Campbell – Author of *Hero of a Thousand Faces*
~

"Julius V is certainly not your mother's Holy Father."
Stephen Coldbeer – Famous Catholic
~

"Holy crap! I'm speechless!"
Pope John XII, Pope Alexander VI and Pope Leo X - Three of the more famous infamous popes
~

"Hell hath no fury like a Sister scorned!"
William Shakespeare – Famous Playwright

To the real Sister LaTrelle. Thank you for taking away my guilt, but not my sins.

Table of Contents

Foreword

I HAD BEEN researching relics of the Catholic Church when I began to study Pope Julius II, a real-life 16th Century pope known as "*Il Papa Terribile*," the Warrior Pope. Could such a man be pope today, I wondered, and could he get away with half the antics Julius II did? "He could if he was the right man and had a prophecy to fulfill," came the answer from the heavens.

So, *Julius V~Warrior Pope* was born and written as a modern action comedy. Hopefully, you'll think it is one. I think you'll enjoy it more with a little background, however. By the way, and I'm sure you know this if you are familiar with the Super Bowl, Julius V is pronounced Julius the Fifth.

Raised by very Catholic parents, I was part of the last generation of American Catholics almost totally educated in grade school by nuns. I was also an altar boy, served a mass for the bishop, and served at a lot of funerals and weddings because I was responsible and my parents made me. Four years of Catholic high school under the whip and tutelage of Benedictine priests also left their marks, some good, some bad, many eye opening.

An early highlight of my upbringing came when I accidently broke a marble holy water fountain right before my First Holy Communion. You can still go to St. Benedict's Church in Atchison, Kansas and see the holy water fountain my dad bought to replace the one I broke. It's off to the side entrance where college students can come inside the church. The fountain that was initially there was moved to the back of the church to replace the one I broke because it matches the others that are there.

How did I break a holy water fountain? By trying to stop a friend's younger brother who was running and screaming in church during a special religious holiday. I chased him down the side aisle and caught him in the back of the church as he made his turn to run up the main aisle again. I grabbed the holy water fountain to stop myself, thinking it was bolted to the floor. It wasn't. I was too small to stop it, although I virtually tossed my tiny body under it to keep it from falling. It crashed to the floor and broke in three equal pieces. It looked as if it had been sawn. Despite getting out of there as fast as my little legs could carry me and biking over a mile home at record speed, my deed had been recorded by something much better than today's surveillance cameras...nearly a hundred pair of eyes of Catholic Faithful. I was soundly busted and forced to do a one-on-one interrogation with the pastor. What I never understood was that no one ever gave me credit for trying to stop a marauding kid from disrupting his or her prayers. But then again I was named after St. Stephen, the "first" martyr, so what do you expect?

I initially wrote Julius V as a screenplay. It has received acclaim from Hollywood insiders for being intelligent, albeit irreverent, comedy. It was also blasted once as being nothing more than a sophomoric attempt at vulgar humor. I prefer the former analysis. Julius V has also been a finalist and semi-finalist in several screenplay contests and took third in the comedy genre of the very competitive 2014 StoryPros Screenplay Contest. I'm still marketing the script to Hollywood, but the ebook version offers extras that aren't possible to deliver in film.

Julius V~Warrior Pope was not written for Catholics or Protestants. It was written for fun. You don't have to be a Christian to either be entertained or put off by Julius V, the book, or by Julius V, the pope. You don't have to be a Catholic or Christian to grasp all the innuendos either. For example, the Prologue strongly emulates the myths of Romulus and Remus, Moses, and Kal-El, the baby who became Superman. In any case, I tried to give enough background so the story flows naturally, but too much information in a story can be too much information. The point is, is that like the Catholic Church, itself, just about everything written in *Julius V~Warrior Pope* has a historical precedence or biblical basis, although comedy tends to highlight certain aspects and down play others.

I hope that is what makes *Julius V~Warrior Pope* entertaining for you.

JULIUS V
WARRIOR POPE

BY

STEVE FRANCIS

Prologue

About Forty Years Ago

EVEN AT THE moment prior to giving birth, Sister Lorraine was gorgeous. Positioned on her hands and knees on a birthing table in a private room in a small convent in rural France, Lorraine sweated profusely. Her dark hair was matted to her head, face, neck and back.

Sister Teresa, the midwife, had her white sleeves rolled up and prepared to catch the child.

Lorraine pushed.

"Beautiful," the midwife said softly.

Lorraine arched her head back and screamed. A baby's head appeared.

Sister Teresa smiled and said, "I'm here, Lorraine. I'm here little one." She held her hands open.

Soon crying was heard. Lorraine smiled and rolled over onto the table. Teresa placed the baby on Lorraine's chest as soon as she could. He was a healthy baby boy.

The other three nuns in the room were pleased and excited. "Oh, he's beautiful," cooed Sister Ann.

"He has his father's eyes," Sister Renée confirmed.

"And your nose," Sister Donna chimed. "Lets get you both cleaned up," said Teresa.

About a half an hour later, the sisters heard heavy footsteps walking in the hall outside the room. The nuns scurried about, not knowing what to do. The door flew open. Two men came in. One wore a suit; the other combat fatigues. The sisters blocked their way.

"No!" screamed Lorraine. Teresa threw the afterbirth and splattered the men.

They pushed her aside and grabbed the newborn.

"The Holy Father commands it," the suit said.

The nuns shrunk back. The men left; the soldier carried the child. He handed him to a nurse who waited outside the room.

A small plane flew over a sunlit and green central Montana. The Musselshell River wound below. Several fringe ranges of snow capped mountains rose in the distance in three directions, breaking up the plains. A small canvas covered bundle dropped from the plane and parachuted toward the river. It descended through the Big Sky and settled easily on the flowing Musselshell. The parachute and cover came off. The bundle was a picnic basket.

The picnic basket floated near a she-cougar drinking at the riverbank. Startled, the cougar took a couple of steps back from the water, then stared intently as the basket drifted closer to her. She heard a baby cry. Her ears perked forward. She drooled. She licked her mouth and whiskers. She stepped gingerly into the river, grabbed the handle of the basket in her teeth and trotted toward a grove of cottonwood trees.

In the shadow of the trees, with the Musselshell River gurgling nearby, the cat put down the basket. Nearby were the limp bodies of her two cougar kittens, killed by a pack of dogs the day before. The bodies of four dogs she killed were partially buried under leaf litter. The she-cougar nimbly lifted the flap of the picnic basket with a paw, then pulled out a blanket. She looked down into the eyes of a little baby boy. He stopped crying, looked up at her and smiled. She gently pulled him out of the basket by his tiny shirt with her teeth. She laid him on the ground and snuggled up to him. He hungrily suckled at one of her teats.

When the boy was satisfied, the cougar picked him up by the back of his shirt as she would a kitten. He dangled from her mouth, laughing, as she returned him to the basket. Then she picked it up and started to trot. She trotted through the afternoon and into the early evening, then lay the boy down and suckled him again. A gurgling sound erupted, this time not from the river, but from the little baby's butt. The cougar scrunched her nose at his stink. She lifted him again and dipped him into the river to clean him. He laughed and splashed in the cold water.

Late that night, the big cat arrived at a small convent. She clawed the door. An inside light came on. The cougar put the basket down in front of her, sat on the porch of the convent and stared at the door.

The porch light came on. A middle-aged nun opened the door and saw the black tip of a cougar's tail flick away into the darkness. She then looked down at the basket on the porch and heard murmuring. And she heard a big cat growl in the night. She peered deeply into the night, but heard nothing more. She lifted the basket's lid and saw the little boy.

"Oh, my goodness! What have we here?"

The baby looked up at her and smiled.

"We need to get you clean and fed," she said. "You stink!"

As the nun brought the baby in the basket inside, she noticed a note pinned to his shirt. She unfastened it and read it. "Oh, my God," she whispered. "Oh, my God."

Chapter I

A Line in the Heavens

About Six Years in the Future

POPE DAMIANO WAS apparently dead. He lay on his back in his bed, naked, but covered from the waist down with a sheet. Even with his mouth slightly open, he looked peaceful. His body was well-muscled for a man of his advanced age.

According to tradition, the Vatican's chamberlain had to make sure the pope had passed. The chamberlain, known as the camerlengo, was Cardinal Rappaporti. He rapped the pontiff's head with a small silver hammer and called out his baptized name.

"Antonio Sole'."

The camerlengo rapped his head again.

"Antonio Sole'."

And one last time, "Antonio Sole', I bid you to awake."

There was no change. Rappaporti pulled his arm all the way back and prepared to smack the pontiff one more time, this time with all his might.

The attending priest put a hand on the cardinal's arm. The cardinal looked at the priest, relaxed and lowered his arm.

Rappaporti addressed the corpse. "OK, Your Holiness. Three strikes and you're out. I pronounce you dead." Rappaporti turned to the priest. "The time?"

"5: 17 a.m.," the priest answered.

"We must let the world know," Rappaporti said.

A young woman dressed in a short bathrobe leaned against a wall and sobbed softly.

Rappaporti looked at her. "Don't worry. His time had come, and evidently so had he."

Ten days later, the College of Cardinals entered the conclave in the Vatican's Sistine Chapel to elect a new pope. The cardinals were in turmoil. Split into two factions, one archconservative and one simply conservative, they argued conflicting and impending prophecies facing the Catholic Church.

"Listen to me," hollered Cardinal Molani above the din. "It has been prophesied that Damiano will be the last pope unless we do something!"

Cardinal Richelieu was old, bent and leaned on a cane. As did the other cardinals, he wore a Pian habit with red sash and buttons, and red zuchetto on his thin, greasy hair.

"The something we must not do is let The Church be controlled by outsiders," Richelieu said. "Otherwise, as St. Malachy forewarned, 'The pope will quit Rome, and in leaving the Vatican, he will have to walk over the dead bodies of his priests.'"

Cardinal Luciani protested. "For God's sakes, Richelieu, The Vatican is built over a cemetery. Everyone who walks here walks over dead bodies of priests. Besides, what are you doing here? The conclave is for cardinals under 80 years old."

Richelieu glared defiantly and said, "I can still be pope."

Conflicting hollers rose up from the cardinals.

"Kick him out!"

"Let him speak!"

"Hold your tongue."

"He has my ear."

"Hold him down!"

"Hear him out!"

"Wash his hair!"

Richelieu scowled. Many of the conservative cardinals shrunk before his glare. He was almost elected pope during the last election, but lost to Antonio Sole', the man who became Pope Damiano. Richelieu still had a strong contingent of archconservative, aging followers, of which he had long been a leader. He leaned on his cane and attempted to straighten his spine and strengthen his voice.

"Heresy is everywhere," he said, wagging a finger at the opposing cardinals, "and the followers of heresy are in power. God will permit a great evil against His Church. Heretics and tyrants will come suddenly and unexpectedly; they will break into the Church ... and defile its treasures."

"Enough!" hollered Rappaporti. "It is time to vote."

"Let's eat first!" a cardinal in the back hollered.

"We vote," Rappaporti said. "It still takes a two-thirds majority to elect a new pope. Let's get to it."

Ballots were passed to the cardinals, completed and placed in a chalice. To assure accuracy, three cardinals tallied the votes.

"I'd like to vote Richelieu off the island," Cardinal Luciani confided to Cardinal Castalleno next to him.

"I'm with you, but it doesn't matter if he stays or goes. He won't be pope," assured Castalleno.

The cardinals voted three more times, but could not agree on a new pope. Hungry and ill tempered, the cardinals called for food. A chef was brought in.

"What's for supper?" the pudgy Cardinal Holman asked.

"Stuffed Lamb of God Chops," replied the chef.

The hungry cardinals rubbed their hands together excitedly.

The chef began to grill chops in the fireplace of the Sistine Chapel. Outside, the anxious crowd in St. Peter's Square looked to the chimney atop the Sistine Chapel for signs of smoke. According to tradition, after the cardinals vote, their ballots are burned in a special furnace in the Sistine Chapel to signal the results to the world. White smoke means a new pope had been elected. Black smoke means no new pope yet. But this time, gray smoke from the grill bellowed out of the Sistine Chapel's chimney. The crowd was confused, unsure of its meaning. Inside the chapel, the cardinals were boisterously happy as they sat down to eat.

After having his fill, Rappaporti put down his napkin and addressed the cardinals. "We must break this impasse."

"That is simple enough. I accept." Richelieu bowed.

The cardinals began to argue again.

One of Richelieu's followers hollered over the others. "For it is written, 'and the great cloud will cause two suns to appear: The big mastiff will howl all night.'"

"Sit down, Bergoni. Night won't be likely with two suns," Cardinal Buunto bellowed.

"There is only one logical choice," Rappaporti countered. "The prophesied dangers are upon us. The Church has reached its nadir. We must elect Damiano's son. He is our salvation."

"He is our demise!" Richelieu howled, slamming the bottom of his cane on the floor. "He's the greatest danger of all!"

"He's fit because of his father." Buunto offered.

"He's unfit because of his father," Richelieu insisted.

"You have no say in this, Dominique," Cardinal Marcherry reasoned.

"I say Damiano's son!" Cardinal Alvarez hollered.

Richelieu and his faction of cardinals wailed in protest. "Woe is me! Woe on us if he is he!"

"Put it to a vote," Cardinal Fritzgerald demanded.

Some hollered and nodded in agreement. Others lamented.

"The sins of the fathers will be visited upon the sons unto the seventh generation," bellowed Cardinal Thorneapple.

Rappaporti called for silence. "This has gone on long enough. We vote again."

Ballots were again passed to the conclave. Three cardinals tallied the votes. When all the votes were counted, Rappaporti addressed the cardinals.

"We have a new pope," he said, stating the obvious.

Jules Sole', the son of the late Pope Damiano Sole' and ostracized parish priest of a small town in Montana, was elected. Rather than cheers, silence filled the Sistine Chapel. Richelieu wrapped a cloak around himself as would a villain and shuffled out of the chapel.

"We've crossed a line in the heavens," said Cardinal Lorenzo.

The cardinals crossed themselves.

Cardinal Rappaporti stepped forward. "Considering the circumstances, we must not yet announce the results of our election. I urge us to send envoys to Father Sole' to let him know of our decision. If God is with us, he will accept."

An anxious crowd in St. Peter's Square looked hopefully to the chimney of the Sistine Chapel for smoke. There was none.

Chapter II

Two Dot

THE VATICAN'S LEAR jet landed on a broken asphalt road outside of Two Dot, Montana. It taxied into town and parked in a weed lot. There were only a few houses, a bar and restaurant, an abandoned bank building, a yellowish two-story garage, the old white hotel in which someone must have lived, and the red shed of the volunteer fire department. The Vatican envoys, Father Carlo and Father Fabio, pressed their faces against the jet windows. They were pasty white, effeminate priests, soft and pampered.

"What a shit hole," Father Carlo said, the shorter of the two.

"I had no idea they had places like this in The States," said Father Fabio.

"Let's find him ..."

"... and get out of here," finished Father Fabio.

"Exactly," affirmed Carlo.

As they deplaned, the envoys were oblivious to the sounds of western meadowlarks, bluebirds and bobolinks singing from the prairie, replete in the spring green that only happened when the grasslands woke up after a cold, snowy winter. They paid no attention to the distant snowcapped mountains that ringed their view beneath impeccable blue skies. They only heard the hammering of steel on steel and saw a man beyond the edge of town at an outdoor smithy. He was the only person around.

The envoys walked the less than two blocks of town toward the man. As they got closer, they noticed a small, immaculate white church flanked by cottonwood and ash trees about a hundred meters from the road.

"This guy should be able to tell us where Father Sole' is," Fabio said.

"Hopefully he's not saying Mass. Nobody else is here," Carlo observed.

The man sweated profusely in his blacksmith apron, heavy pants, boots and gloves. Muscular and focused, he whistled happily as he shaped a red-hot horseshoe and tempered it in a steamy water bath. As they got closer, the priests saw sweat drip from the man's forehead and thick black and gray hair. His sweat and the steam met somewhere in the hot air around him.

A finely muscled stallion gracefully strolled about the grounds that included randomly placed archery targets pocked with holes. The horse's gold metallic coat shimmered in the morning sun. A superior specimen, even among the Akhal-Teke, a breed of tall, powerful and intelligent animals, Eli was a horse fit for a king.

To the envoys' surprise, the smithy, an open barn and nearby grounds had the order and feel of a perfect sanctuary, despite the third world mystique of the town. All unused tools were clean and organized on the walls. Horse tack was stored neatly. The stalls and floor were clean. The smell was rich and earthy, mixed with the smell and sounds of hot steel. The horse stopped, picked up his ears and watched the envoys. The man continued to work as the two approached him. He pounded on another piece of hot steel.

Putti, small cherubic angels often depicted naked, or slightly robed, in Renaissance paintings and sculptures, flew around the blacksmith. The blacksmith, but no one else, could see and hear them, although he seldom paid attention. One putto frequently wore a red mask and had red wings. The other had a halo and white rings.

Father Fabio hollered out, "Excuse me."

The white putto's wings beat merrily as he said, "Jules, you have company."

The red putto flapped next to the white one and admonished, "Don't spoil the surprise."

The man stayed focused on his work, but replied to the putti, "I'm busy. Go."

The putti poofed away. The envoys came closer.

"Excuse me," Fabio repeated.

He tentatively tapped the blacksmith on the shoulder. The blacksmith quickly turned, stepped on the man's foot as he pushed him against a wall with his left hand. His right hand aimed hot forge tongs at Fabio's throat. The blacksmith quickly discerned these men were no threat.

"Oops. So sorry. Can I help you?" The man lowered his tongs. And removed his earplugs. "I can't hear a thing with these in. Besides, no one ever comes out here when I work, let alone priests."

Both envoys were terrified and froze. The blacksmith pulled Fabio from the wall and straightened his shirt.

"I really am sorry. What can I do for you?" he asked.

The envoys just stared, speechless. The blacksmith peered around them and saw the tail and part of the cabin of the Lear parked in the grass across town.

"Did you drive that here?" he asked, then turned away and got a ladle of water from a bucket.

Father Carlo finally spoke. "Do you know where we can find Father Jules?"

"Call me Jules," the blacksmith said. He took a drink from the ladle. The horse was at a trough and also started to drink.

"We're from The Vatican," Carlo said.

Fabio chimed in. "From the College of Cardinals, actually. You've been elected pope."

Jules blew water out of his nose and mouth. Outside, the horse snorted water out of his nose, shook his head and trotted uneasily in circles.

Jules called to the horse. "Easy, Eli."

Eli slowed down, snorted again and walked toward the smithy.

Jules glared at the envoys. Both raised their hands in defense. The body odor from Jules made their eyes water.

"Now, now. Don't kill the messengers," Fabio said.

"Get out," Jules said plainly and softly.

The envoys backed away. Unknown to them, Eli was right behind them. Suddenly, he neighed and reared. Terrified at Eli's flaying hoofs, they ran out of the smithy toward the plane. Eli trotted behind them, nosing their butts to keep them stumbling toward the Lear. They ran up the stairs and into the plane, pulling the door closed behind them. Eli trotted back toward Jules, with his head and tail held high.

Jules pulled off his apron and gloves and swung up on Eli. Eli needed no urging to gallop into the rolling hills of central Montana.

Father Carlo called Cardinal Rappaporti. "We found him," the priest reported.

"And?" asked Rappaporti.

"He said no."

"I figured as much." Rappaporti paused. "Promise him anything he wants. We need him!"

"We'll talk to him again in the morning."

"Talk to him now," Rappaporti growled.

"He just rode off on a wild horse," Carlo explained. "Not even the Lear could catch them."

"Promise him anything," Rappaporti reminded Carlo, and then hung up the phone. To himself he said, "His father was incorrigible. Jules promises to be even worse."

Jules rode back to the barn after dark. He rubbed Eli down and put him in the round pen. Jules put gear away and walked across the grounds to the cottage near the church. Owls hooted in the cottonwoods and nighthawks called overhead, silhouetted against the stars. Beaver thumped their tails on the water as they dove below the surface of the Musselshell River.

Inside the cottage kitchen Jules got a beer. After tossing leftover meat and beans into a pot to heat, he walked into the living room, turned on a low light and sat in the large brown recliner, which took up more of the small room than a chair should. He drank and thought.

"Crazy bastards. Me. Pope. Jesus Christ."

The back door opened. Jules rested comfortably as a man entered.

"Hello, Father."

"Mark. Grab yourself, and a beer, and join me."

"OK." Mark got a beer out of the refrigerator and sat down near the priest. "What's that plane doing out there?"

"You wouldn't believe it if I told you. Care to stay for supper?"

"No thanks. I just want to tell you I finished the painting."

Jules sprang out of his chair. "Already? Let's have a look!"

The men walked outside with beers in hand. They saw the Lear across town in the moonlight, with some of its cabin lights on.

"So really, what's going on with the plane?"

"It's from The Vatican. They sent a couple of lackeys to tell me I've been elected pope."

"That's great!"

Jules took a drink. "That's wrong. Goes to show you how messed up those people are."

"So they sent a plane to take you to Rome?"

"I'm not going to Rome. This is home."

"Then what are they still doing here?"

"Waiting for the tower to clear them for take off, I guess," Jules said.

"If you were pope, they couldn't keep you out of the Julius II Games."

Jules looked hard at Mark, then laughed "I hadn't thought of that."

They walked down the cellar steps of the chapel and turned on light switches. Track lights focused on an easel. Mark walked to it and pulled off its cloth cover. He revealed the painting to Jules, an exact replica of the Renaissance artist, Raphael's masterpiece portrait of Pope Julius II.

"My God! You are a modern Renaissance man. Look at this. It's perfect." Jules paced back and forth in front of the portrait as he admired it. "He's the kind of pope The Vatican needs, the world needs."

"Then why don't you take the job?"

"I could never fill his tiara." Jules appraised the portrait again." You did an excellent job showing his remorse for losing the City of Bologna in battle. Even when he lost, the man was a winner!"

"It's late, Jules. I need to get home to the wife. Where would you like the painting?"

"I'll take it. Go home. Tell Margaret I said 'Hi.' He handed Mark a wad of money. "Good night."

Mark looked at the bills. "This is a lot more than we agreed on."

"Keep it," Jules said with a smile. "I did exceptionally well betting on the horses over the weekend."

After supper and cognac, Jules took the portrait of Julius II upstairs to his room. He showered, then toweled off in front of the portrait. He adjusted a light to highlight the painting more.

"If I didn't like you so much I'd send you back to Rome with those two clowns and say 'Here's your pope,'" he said to the painting.

Jules glanced out his bedroom window and saw the Lear.

"I'll take care of them in the morning," he said to himself. "Too tired now."

He hung up the towel, slipped on a pair of boxers, got into bed and turned off the light. The whoo-whoooo of great horned owls along the Musselshell, crickets and a slight breeze rustling the leaves of the ash and cottonwood trees near his house lulled Jules into deep relaxation. Moonlight came through the window. It highlighted the portrait. Jules slept without noticing. The putti hovered above him.

"I'm telling ya," the white putto said, "our man needs to go to Rome and save The Church."

"To hell with The Church," the red putto replied. "Can you imagine the women he'd save?"

"Get your mind out of the gutter. Our man's as pure as the driven snow."

"Ha! You saw him when he was younger. The only prophecy he believed in then was: 'And he shall rule them with a rod of iron.'"

The painting begins to talk. "That sounds like me when I was pope, now get out of the way."

The putti scurried over the bed at the sound of the voice and cried out together, "It's Pope Julius!"

A phantom-like figure appeared above the sleeping Jules.

"So, you don't want to follow in your father's footsteps, eh?" the phantom Julius II said sarcastically. "You prefer to horse around Bumfuck, Montana rather than play the game you were meant for? You haven't been banished, asshole, you've been brainwashed. Go to the Vatican. I need you."

Jules stirred within his dream and muttered, "Why me?"

Julius II snarled, "Why the hell not?"

Restless, Jules muttered again, "Why now?"

Julius II was impatient. "Oh, for Christ's sakes. You need more reasons? Because your father was pope. Because it's possible to be a lover and a fighter," Julius II laughed, "and a pope! Believe me, no one dead or alive appreciates me more than you. Hell, I'd still be pope if I were alive today, but as I'm not, you're the only one who can stop what needs to stop and start what needs to start. That's why."

The phantom floated down to Jules' ear. "In the morning those two jokers are coming back with an offer. Before the cock crows three times, here's what I want you to say ..."

Jules woke up to the crow of a neighbor's rooster and rubbed his head. He realized he was hearing knocking on the front door. He pulled on shorts, went downstairs and saw the two Vatican priests at the door. He opened it.

"Come in," he said flatly. "I can't talk until I have coffee." He pointed toward the kitchen.

The two sat down at the kitchen table. Jules began to make coffee. Father Carlo began to speak.

Jules, with his back to them, held up a hand and said, "Shhhh. No talking."

The two men looked at each other as the coffee dripped. Jules stared out the window with his back to the two. Sunlight kissed the tops of the cottonwood trees by the stream running through the grounds, and the prairie on the surrounding hills. Meadowlarks and horned larks sang nonstop in the fields. Robins and rabbits hopped along the ground under the trees near the house. Jules struggled to remember something from a dream from the night before.

Father Fabio attempted to speak. "Father ..."

Jules again held up a hand without turning around. "Shhhh."

Finches, wrens and sparrows sang and flittered among the bird feeders and statues of St. Francis and fairies in the yard. Whitetail deer walked furtively among the cottonwoods. When the coffee was done, Julius poured three cups. After Julius had a cup he looked at the priests.

"Why are you still here?" he asked.

Carlo and Fabio looked at each other before Fabio answered, "To take you to Rome. If you accept, you can have anything you want: money, women, men, boys. Anything."

"Anything?" Jules asked.

Carlo and Fabio looked at each other again, nodded, then back to Julius and together repeated, "Anything."

Jules got up absently and opened the kitchen door. Eli opened the gate of the round pen with his mouth, walked up the patio to the door and stood face to face with Jules. Jules breathed in Eli's horse scent and other morning smells. He felt compelled to ask for something, something that was just out of reach. He put his hands on Eli's face, then he heard the rooster crow a second time.

Jules turned back to the priests. Without thinking he said, "I want to be crowned pope with the Tiara of Julius II while on horseback."

The two priests looked surprised. "Surely you jest," Fabio responded softly.

Jules was relieved. "I know. It's too much. So, thank you gentlemen. Have a good flight home."

"No, that's fine," Carlo interceded. "We can do that."

"Really?" asked Jules.

Fabio clapped his hands and smiled. "Done!" he said. "Anything else?"

"And the Julius II Games go on a year from September, as planned," Jules said.

"Of course, Your Holiness," Carlo beamed.

"Please ... don't call me that," Jules said, sensing change, for better or for worse. "Looks as if you just bought yourself a pope."

The putti were ecstatic.

"Woo-hoo! We're going to The Vatican!" the white putto exclaimed.

"Where the living is easy!" the red putto chimed.

The cock crowed the third time.

Jules and Gino, the Lear pilot spent a couple of hours that morning getting the plane ready for Eli, bolting in tie-downs for cargo netting to keep Eli secure. Jules called Mark to tell him he was leaving. Mark's wife, Margaret, Jules' part time secretary, spread the word to Jules' parishioners, although where and why Jules was leaving was to be kept secret. But, besides Mark and Margaret, there was one other person to whom Jules wanted to tell the whole story. He got on his motorcycle.

Jules rode east along the river towards Lavina. Near town, he stopped at a small building, trotted up the porch and saw the cat claw marks still on the door after all the years. As was his custom, he touched them. Then he looked around the corner of the porch to the backyard. An old barefoot woman tended marijuana plants in a greenhouse. She looked out the door, smiled and slightly lifted the floral dress that went to her shins as she came quickly to him.

"Jules," Sister Grace said warmly with shiny eyes. Before Jules could answer, she said, "Oh, they've come for you."

"Ah, you know," Jules said.

"Of course," the old woman said.

"But not with the pitch fork you warned me about!" he said.

"Oh, they sent real devils," she laughed.

"How did you know?" Jules asked.

"I can read any man by the look in his eye, which is probably why I never married," she said. "When do you leave?"

"As soon as I get back."

She nodded. She took Jules' arm. "I knew it was just a matter of time before they called you in. Do you have time for a drink?"

"That's why I'm here," Jules answered.

The two walked to the backyard. A bottle of Patrón sat in the shade of a table umbrella.

"How are your plants?" Julius asked, nodding to the greenhouse.

"Let me put it this way," the old nun said as she poured a couple of shots of tequila. "Those coffee-roasting Carmelite monks in Wyoming leave a lot of money on the table by not doing what I do."

Jules laughed as the two clinked glasses.

Then Grace added, "Personally, I find that being a grower keeps me closer to God."

Jules slowly spun the glass in his hands. "Grace, I want to thank you again for saving my life and taking care of me. I've asked before, so I'll ask again. How can I repay you?" he asked.

Grace smiled lovingly. "Aside from keeping the DEA away, just give your mother my love."

Jules looked shocked. "What?"

Grace went inside and quickly came back with a small box. "You've known for a long time who your father was," she said. "I wouldn't keep that from you, but I didn't tell you about your mother because she was afraid they'd hurt you and I was afraid they'd hurt her if you found out." Grace handed the box to Jules and said, "This note was pinned to you the night the cat brought you to me. It's from your mother. She was able to get it to someone who dropped you out of that plane. That's how I knew who your father was long before he came looking for you."

"I wish he'd have never found me."

"Fortunately, by the time he did, you were old enough to stand up to him. Most people couldn't."

Jules smiled. "I still don't know if I became a priest to impress him or piss him off. Either way, it cost me."

"And he could never decide the best way to muck up your life," Grace added.

"I'd say he did a pretty good job." Jules opened the box and unfolded the note. It was the first time he'd seen his mother's handwriting. He studied the note, tossed back another shot of tequila and asked, "How'd the two of them get together?"

"It wasn't consensual. He kept your mother a virtual prisoner at the Vatican before and after you were born."

"He told me she died," Jules said.

"She is indomitable."

"He was a prick."

Grace laughed hard. " I know! Great at changing his mind, but not his heart. Keep the note. It'll prove to your mother you are her son, not that a son ever needs to prove who he is to his mother. She and I have been great pen pals over the years."

When Jules got back to Two Dot early that afternoon, hundreds of people from throughout central Montana were waiting. Old men, young women and teenage girls were teary and reserved. Pick up trucks were lined along

Highway 12 and through Two Dot. The Lear was blocked in. The envoys were anxious.

"We need to go, Father," Fabio said.

Jules patted him on the shoulder as he turned to Mark. "I'll come back when I can," he said to Mark. The men embraced.

Jules hugged and kissed Margaret and a few other close friends. He took Eli's reins from a cowboy and walked the horse up a ramp to the Lear's doorway. He turned back to the people.

"I really do love you all," he said. "Thank you for letting me be your priest."

Julius and Eli disappeared inside the plane. People moved their cars and trucks, and the Lear taxied through town as it prepared to take off. Soon it was airborne and flying east, with the Musselshell flowing below it.

Chapter III

Julius V

THE LEAR TOUCHED down at Rome's Leonardo da Vinci airport in the dark of the early morning. A white Mercedes pulled up to the plane. The envoys appeared at the top of the ramp of the Lear's doorway and stiffly hobbled down it. Jules nimbly followed them with Eli. The men got in the car. A white Mercedes van pulled a horse trailer with Eli.

Fabio talked into his cell phone. "We'll be there in 30 minutes."

Soon, the Mercedes and van came into view of Vatican City. St. Peter's Square was full of people awaiting the election of a new pope. Rabid Catholics lobbied for their preferred papal candidates. They carried signs and called out the names of their favorites. Swiss Vatican Guards, dressed in their daily solid dark blue uniforms, with black boots and berets, managed the crowd.

Both Mercedes circled the Vatican wall around St. Peter's Square and stopped at the back of the Sistine Chapel. Vatican guards opened the car's doors. The priests got out and, under escort, walked inside a hall leading to the Sistine Chapel. Two guards, dressed in their formal blue, red and yellow uniforms and white gloves, stood at the chapel doors.

Carlo spoke to Jules. "This is where we leave you, Your Holiness." He held out his hand.

Jules shook the priest's hand as he said, "Really, you don't have to call me that."

Fabio offered his hand as well and said, "It's been a pleasure, Your Holiness. And remember, you can trust Sarge."

Jules took his hand. "And remember you promised to show me around Rome," he said with a smile.

The envoys agreed, then Carlo nodded to the Post Sergeant, who ordered two Vatican guards to open the door. Julius walked inside and immediately stared starry-eyed at the famous ceiling.

"Ah, Michelangelo and Julius II. What a team," he commended, referring to Julius II commissioning Michelangelo to paint the chapel. Then Jules felt the eyes upon him. He looked around the chapel.

The cardinals were in various sized groups. They were also of various sizes and colors: short, tall, fat, white, black, brown. Most were very soft. As they became aware that Jules was in the chapel, they slowly quit talking to one another. In silence, they appraised Jules. A few began to whisper.

"He looks like his father."

"And his mother."

Jules appraised the cardinals in return. "Let's have a drink," Jules said and smiled.

"He acts like his father."

"And hospitable, like his mother."

"He looks stronger than he did before."

"Well, he's been in Montana, U.S.A."

"After what his father did, he must be pissed."

"I pray he's learned forgiveness."

Cardinal Rappaporti walked forward, in a manner that said he was used to being in charge. He faced Jules, who stood at least five inches taller than the cardinal.

"We need to make this official," Rappaporti said. "Father Jules Sole', do you accept your canonical election as Supreme Pontiff?"

"You are?" Jules asked, holding Rappaporti's gaze until the cardinal looked away.

Rappaporti was not used to priests questioning him. "The man responsible for bringing you here, Cardinal Joseph Rappaporti. Your father was a good friend."

"And my mother?"

"She was a good friend of your father's, too."

Jules turned abruptly and started to walk out of the chapel.

"Please, Father Jules, wait," Rappaporti implored sincerely. We really do need you. Will you accept the papacy?"

Jules calmed down and remembered his dream. "If you accept my terms. I have to be crowned with ..."

Rappaporti slipped back into his curt demeanor and cut Jules off with a wave of his hand. "Yes. Yes. Yes. Your 'terms' are accepted."

"This is a travesty!" hollered Richelieu.

Jules looked at him, laughed and asked, "Who are you?"

Rappaporti faced Richelieu. "Francois, I will have you carried out of here bodily if you don't shut up. You've had your say. There's too much at stake now." He pointed to Jules. "No one else can protect us from ourselves now or protect us from what might be coming. Get over it and yourself."

Richelieu's beet red face twisted sadistically. Spit splattered on the ornately designed marble floor. Cardinals looked at him in disgust, especially the ones with phlegm-splattered black shoes.

"For god's sakes, Richelieu, get a hold of yourself," Cardinal Luzano admonished. "You never cared about this so much before."

"He's unfit ... because of his father!" Richelieu raved, pointing at Jules.

"I take that as a compliment," Jules added.

"He's fit because of his father!" Gilbersven shot back at Richelieu.

"I'm certainly more fit than you," Jules said to the marshmallow-bellied man.

"Enough!" bellowed Rappaporti. "We may be assailed as we dally."

Television reporters cruised St. Peter's Square, anticipating the crowd's reaction to another vote. Many eyes were on the chimney.

Cable television's People's Analysis of God's Announcements Network, known as PAGAN, was a major player in covering Vatican news. Lisa and Neil, the network's top news analysts, sat at an elevated news desk slightly above the crowd. Young, attractive and upbeat, the commentating couple frequently competed against each other on the air for camera time.

Looking at the camera, Lisa said, "Rumors of a mystery man, a mystery priest, abound in St. Peter's Square. The papal Lear landed at Leonardo da Vinci airport and a white Mercedes immediately drove from there to the back of the Sistine Chapel, circumventing the Vatican Museums, so as not to have to pay the museum fee. And, more mysteriously, a Mercedes van was pulling a white horse trailer."

Neil interjected, "Let's be responsible, Lisa. A horse trailer could be hauling camels or an elephant. We might just as easily have an Imam or Swami as pope."

Lisa was unperturbed. "There is no indication from where the Lear flew. No Italian at the control tower will talk, not even with his hands."

"We all know the Catholic Church has its issues," said Neil.

"Hell, it's in crisis," chimed Lisa.

"True. It'll take more than a miracle to return to Paradise," Neil added.

Lisa nodded her head of thick blond hair as she said. "The Times they are a changin'."

"To every season, turn, turn, turn," Neil said.

Back inside the Sistine Chapel, Rappaporti affirmed Jules acceptance by asking, "By what name will you be known?"

"Julius," Jules replied.

Rappaporti looked at Jules blankly, as if he'd been shot. Some of the cardinals moaned, others laughed. A few backslapped their friends as a cacophony broke out.

"Really? Another Julius?"

"Oh, no."

"Could be worse than his father."

"Or better."

"Can certainly be no worse than Julius II."

"Or no better?"

"But look at this place. Julius II is responsible for it."

"So is Michelangelo."

"It'd never happen again." "

Although we may need one."

"Another warrior pope or a Sistine Chapel?"

"Hopefully neither."

"Or both."

"At least he won't ride a horse inside, the way Julius II did."

"Don't be so sure."

"His father never even did that."

"Don't be so sure."

"I say, 'What the hell? Give him a chance.'"

"What do you think his mother will say?"

"I don't know, but I'd love to be there when they meet."

Richelieu was livid. He hollered above the din. "Really? Another Julius? Is there no end to this farce? This fiasco?"

"Let's turn it into a fresco," Luciano said, pointing to the ceiling.

Rappaporti turned to the new pope. "May I?" he asked, almost deferentially, as he nodded toward Richelieu.

Sensing Rappaporti's intent, Julius responded, "Please do."

As Rappaporti strutted to the large door of the Sistine Chapel, he called over his shoulder, "That's it, Francois. I've had enough of you." He opened the door and looked out as he pointed inside at Richelieu. "Sergeant, carry this man out!"

The sergeant, Kaspar Von Soldaten, also known simply as Sarge, called for two Vatican guards to enter the chapel with him. Terrified, Richelieu looked for a way to escape. There was none. Too feeble and slow to resist, Richelieu tried to threaten them with his cane, but lost his balance, falling into the arms of the guards.

"Take him to the kitchen," Rappaporti ordered. "Tell Sister Lorraine to watch him!"

The guards lifted Richelieu by his feet and ankles. His joints popped as they carried him out of the chapel.

The cardinals watched as Richelieu raised his head and screamed, "Put me down! This is no way to treat a man of the cloth."

The guards carried Richelieu out of the chapel and the big doors closed behind them. The cardinals within the chapel heard Richelieu scream, "Joseph, go to hell! Each and every one of you, go to hell!"

The atmosphere within the Sistine immediately mellowed. A feeling of harmony between the factions ensued. Rappaporti walked to a furnace and stooped toward the door.

Julius peered over Rappaporti's shoulder and said, "That looks like a still. What's it for?"

"That's where the ballots are burned. Black smoke tells the faithful we haven't elected a pope yet. White smoke says we have. Today, you're the man! The army gives us flares so we send up the right color of smoke. But I can't get the door open. We've had trouble with it."

"Let me see," Julius said. He squatted and studied the front of the stove. "The furnace door latch is jammed." Julius took out his Leatherman multitool and adjusted a few screws. He turned the handle and the door popped open. "There we go. Now what do you want to burn?"

The Cardinals gathered up their ballots and brought them over to Julius.

"You probably shouldn't do this," Cardinal Gilbersven offered. "I don't know if a pope has ever lit his own signal fire before."

"I don't mind," Julius said with a smile.

Julius wadded up a ballot, scraped some shavings onto it from his firestarter, then struck a spark on it with the back of his knife. He blew on the smoking ballot and soon a flame was burning. Gilbersven handed Julius a few more ballots. After Julius got those burning, he added the rest of them.

"What color of smoke do you want?" Julius asked Rappaporti.

"White. You're pope now."

"Oh, right. Hand me one of those white flares."

Rappaporti did. Julius popped it and tossed it into the furnace, then closed the door.

"All that's left to do is make you Bishop of Rome, and you're good to go," Richelieu said, trying to be deferential.

Outside in St. Peter's Square, reporters and believers kept watch on the chimney of the Sistine Chapel in the night.

"We just received word that yet another vote was held," said Lisa. "We don't know the outcome yet, but as are thousands of faithful, our eyes are on the chimney of the Sistine Chapel, as if awaiting for a sign from heaven."

"There is nothing coming out of it yet," added Neil, "but the color of the chimney's smoke tells us whether or not a new pope has been elected."

"Rumors continue to persist of the election of an outsider," Lisa added. "And, not long ago, Vatican guards were seen carrying out a black body bag, heightening speculation that one newly elected pope may have already been murdered."

"They did take the body to the Vatican Kitchen, which is where they do autopsies," said Neil.

"No wonder this crowd is so agitated, well in excess of 150,000 people. Oh, look!" exclaimed Lisa. "Smoke is starting to come out of the Sistine chimney. I believe it's white!"

"Let's be sure of what we're seeing here, Lisa. We've made mistakes before," cautioned Neil.

The crowd looked toward the chimney. "It's white!" someone called.

People jumped up and down, screamed, crossed themselves and hugged each other.

"That smoke is definitely white," Lisa said. "We have a winner!"

"As long as the guards don't carry out another body bag, we do," added Neil.

The large bells atop St. Peter's Basilica swung into action.

"That's the distinctive ringing known as "The Whole Peal," said Lisa. "The new pope should appear soon at the Central Balcony of St. Peter's Basilica."

The newly minted Pope Julius V walked out of the Sistine Chapel. The guards at the door snapped to attention. Julius smiled and blessed them, then whistled. Eli, waiting patiently inside the doublewide horse trailer, lifted his head and stuck it out the back of the trailer. He released the door latch with his mouth. He trotted toward the chapel.

As he saw Eli come through the hall, one of the Swiss guards exclaimed, "Mein Gott! Vot a horse!"

Cardinal Rappaporti came out as Eli arrived at the chapel door.

"This is quite extraordinary, Your Holiness," said Rappaporti.

"I'd feel like an idiot standing on the balcony doing that papal wave," Julius said, as he affectionately stroked Eli's head with the other. "It works for some, my father, for example, but not for me. Besides, I don't want to ride Eli up the stairs. I just put new shoes on him; he'd scratch the tile. How much time do you need?"

"Maybe ten minutes," answered Rappaporti.

"Perfect," Julius answered. Julius grabbed Eli's mane and pulled himself up on Eli bareback. Eli pranced slightly, easily carrying the new pope.

"I'll see you in the square then," Rappaporti said.

As Rappaporti left, the rest of the cardinals cheered Julius and smiled. Julius raised his hip flask to them, was going to take a drink, but then thought better of it and put the flask away.

Cardinal Rappaporti strode into St. Peter's Basilica with an assistant, Monsignor Tupelli, at his side. "I have second doubts about this guy already. I hope we didn't make a mistake."

"What are you going to do about Cardinal Richelieu?" asked Tupelli.

"Just keep him in the kitchen overnight to calm him down. He's an embarrassment, not a threat ... and hopefully a bigger mistake than this Pope Julius."

Neil spoke as the television camera focused on the empty Central Balcony of St. Peter's Basilica above the crowd. "We expect to see and hear from Cardinal Rappaporti soon to announce the new pope to the world."

"The people continue to cheer madly. I don't know who or what they expect, but they are ecstatic, nevertheless," Lisa added.

"There's Cardinal Rappaporti at the balcony now," Neil said, unable to contain all of his excitement. "Let's listen as he speaks the traditional words to acknowledge a new pope."

"I bring you tidings of great joy," Rappaporti said in Latin. "We have a new Pope, His Holiness, Pope Julius V, formerly known as Father Jules Sole'."

Lisa and Neil turned to each other, then quickly scanned their list of top papal candidates. "Do we have the translation right? We don't seem to have any information on a Father Jules Sole'," said Neil.

Lisa gazed around St. Peter's Square. "The crowd seems a bit bewildered. The Papal Shield is on a tapestry and being hung over the rail of the balcony."

"We expect to see the new pontiff any time next to the cardinal," Neil said. "He should have been fitted with his new vestments by now, traditionally a white "skullcap" or zucchetto, and white vestments. Meanwhile, we'll try to get some info on this mystery pontiff."

Lisa quickly skimmed a piece of paper and said, "Neil, I just got a message from one of our researchers. Julius V is the bastard son of the late Pope Damiano I, whose birth name was Antonio Sole'. The new pontiff was neither a cardinal nor a bishop, but a simple parish priest in Two Dot, Montana, U.S.A. This has to be one of the biggest surprises in papal history."

"I'm getting more info, too, Lisa. Father Jules was the mystery man flown in earlier today. It's difficult to say what would possess the Conclave to elect what ostensibly is an embarrassment to the Church, other than this new pontiff can't be any more of an embarrassment than the Church has been to itself."

"And," added Lisa, "seemingly his own father exiled him to Montana after Father Jules won the horseback archery competition at the Pope Julius II Games nearly three years ago. Before that, he had a small parish in Macedonia, where he excelled at gambling and horsemanship. Supposedly he asked for that post after serving in France's Alsace Province in his early days as a priest. And he moonlighted as an actor while studying at a seminary in France. That's all we have on him."

"No information even on where he was born or how old he is?" Neil asked.

Lisa shook her head no and added, "Truly strange."

"He may be unknown and unqualified, but he doesn't seem to be vilified, except the fact he's a bastard," observed Neil.

"When you pick a pope, that's the lesser of two evils," Lisa agreed.

The cameras turned back to the crowd in the square as Lisa continued. "The people near the bottom of the stairs to St. Peter's Basilica are more excited. Some are jumping up and down and pointing, not at the balcony, but at the top of the stairs," she said.

Neil got up from his chair. "Something unusual is going on. I see a man on a horse riding in front of the façade of St. Peter's. Vatican guards are on the steps below, keeping the crowd at bay," he said.

As a camera brought the rider up close on a monitor, Lisa exclaimed, "By Jove, Neil, I think he's our boy! I've just been handed a picture of Father Jules. What a stud!"

"We better call him Pope Julius if he's as good with that bow as the reports say he is," Neil cautioned.

Julius cantered Eli back and forth at the top of the stairs and waved to the crowd, with no papal gestures. Smiling broadly, Julius doffed his white papal skullcap. People jumped up and down.

"The pope seems to have told the Vatican guards to let the people through, as a throng is now running up the stairs toward him," observed Neil.

Eli walked slowly as Julius leaned over touching and blessing the people. When an old woman was finally able to make her way to him, he gave her his skullcap and kissed her on the cheek. She touched his and smiled with tears in her eyes. Spotlights careened around the square, bouncing light around the buildings.

Crowd noise almost drowned out Lisa and Neil. They shouted into their microphones.

"This is a big night for the Catholic Church, the people in St. Peter's and Catholics around the world," Lisa said.

"It's got to be big for Pope Julius V, as well," added Neil.

"You're on your own, Neil. I'm going to ask him to sign my Gideon bible." Lisa sprang from the announcer's deck and into the crowd, with a bible tucked under her arm. Neil watched Lisa's thick blond hair bob through the crowd as she forced her way toward Julius.

"I wonder what the new pope will do when he reads what I wrote in her bible," Neil commented with a wry smile to the television audience.

Chapter IV

Reunion

SISTER LORRAINE MOPPED the Vatican kitchen floor and watched the television as Pope Julius V rode Eli amidst the adoring crowd before St. Peter's Basilica. The smooth skin of her small forearms rippled with muscle as she squeezed the mop in the wringer. She was so full of adrenaline that the mop was virtually dry after every squeeze.

She finished the floor as the new pope gave a final wave to the crowd, then he disappeared behind the Basilica façade. Lorraine opened a closet door, put away the bucket and hung the mop next to a black body bag squirming on a peg. She went back to the television. A photo of the new pope was now on the screen. Her mother's heart tugged toward her son. She had not been this close to him since the day he was born.

"He looks like his father," the little nun said, "but doesn't act like him. Thank god."

As Julius disappeared from the crowd, Sarge stayed close. He already felt an overwhelming sense of loyalty to Julius, beyond anything required of his oath to protect him. Julius dismounted and turned to Sarge. Julius' eyes were both shining and teary.

"Will you take me to the kitchen?" Julius asked.

"Of course, Your Holiness. I was going to suggest it," the soldier replied. "And Nils can take care of your horse," he added, signaling one of his men over.

"I can board him in the Vatican Gardens shop, Your Holiness," Nils said. "He will be out of the weather and given feed and water."

Julius handed the reins to Nils. "Perfect. Thank you," he added with a smile.

Eli and Nils walked toward the lush grounds of the Vatican Gardens. Julius and Sarge walked in the dark between tight clusters of buildings toward the kitchen. Julius was lost in thought about his mother. He hadn't been this close to her since the day he was born.

"Do you know Sister Lorraine?" Julius asked.

"I do," Sarge replied. "She's been a favorite of every Vatican guard for over forty years. She's tough as nails, happy as a clam, a better cook than Julia Child – she keeps Julia's picture up in the cafeteria instead of the pope's – sings as well as any preacher's daughter, and mothers us better than could Mother Theresa ... unless you mess in her kitchen. She's a lot prettier, too."

Julius stopped at the kitchen's backdoor.

"Thank you, Sarge," he said with a smile.

Sarge saluted, slapping a forearm across his chest and snapping his heels together. "God bless, Your Holiness," he said and held open the door for Julius.

Julius squeezed Sarge's shoulder and walked inside.

"Whoever that is, you better wipe your feet! I just mopped the floor," boomed a voice.

Julius smiled. "So this is what it's like to have a mother," he said quietly to himself.

Julius wiped his feet, checked his boots and wiped them again. He dried his sweaty palms on his pants. Satisfied, he walked through the cloakroom toward the main light of the kitchen. The teeniest nun he'd even seen was on a ladder, hanging large kettles on pegs above the stove. She had her back to him. He paid little attention to a smell he knew well.

"If you're hungry, there's leftover chicken cacciatore in the refrigerator, but it's still warm," the nun said without looking.

Julius said the first words that came to his head. "I just flew in from Montana. Thought I'd stop in and introduce myself."

The little nun froze. Then she turned over her left shoulder, saw Julius, lost her balance and fell. Julius was under her in a flash. He caught her in his arms.

"Hi, mom," he said with a smile as they looked into each other's eyes.

Lorraine buried her face in his chest. "You adorable bastard," she said and sobbed uncontrollably for a bit.

Julius rocked her.

When she gathered her composure, Lorraine wiped her eyes. "You can put me down now," she said.

She pulled out a couple of chairs at a table for them and asked, "How about some pie?"

"What kind?"

"Huckleberry."

"Where did you find huckleberries in Italy?" Julius asked as he laughed.

"Sister Grace had your friend, Mark, put some on your plane so I could make you your favorite pie. It's in the oven. Didn't you see white smoke coming out of the chimney before you came in?"

As Julius looked toward the oven, he caught sight of the large photo of Julia Child hanging on the wall above a stainless steel counter. Lorraine followed his gaze.

"I named you Jules after her," she said.

Julius laughed again. "You named me after a cook?"

"Yes, and it seems you named yourself Julius after her, too."

"I named myself after a pope," Julius corrected with mock reproach. "By the way, aren't you supposed to have a picture of the pope there rather than her?"

Lorraine laughed. "Not in the kitchen. I'm not interested in recipes for disaster."

"Speaking of disaster, where's Cardinal Richelieu," Julius asked.

Lorraine pointed. "In the closet." The timer on the oven rang. "Let's have pie and catch up before we let him out."

Chapter V

R & R

OVER THE NEXT sixteen months, Julius became acquainted with the rigor and ritual and routine of the papacy, its idiosyncrasies and personalities. He was very good at listening to advice, although not always good at taking it. His boundless energy and easy demeanor made him a star with the media, political leaders, religious leaders of all beliefs, and Christians and non-Christians alike. As Pope Julius V, he retained most of the staff of his father. He wasn't he happy with the State of the Church, but took little interest in daily operations except for the most important of all ... The Julius II Games. And, as Jules Sole', he often took late night solo sojourns. It was as likely to see him at the theater, as it was playing beach volleyball under the lights. The putti had predicted correctly. The living was easy.

Under a warm, morning Mediterranean sun in the Vatican Gardens, Julius conducted his weekly audience near the *Fontana dell'Aquilone*, the Fountain of the Eagle. He enjoyed these immensely.

The theme that sunny day was wealth and possession. Julius sat in a circle with the people on the grass. He wore what had become his trademark black gabardine pants and a flowing beige shirt. In his usual custom, Julius answered questions from, rather than preached to, the people.

"Most Holy Father," a pious looking young man said, "for years I've heard and read this from the bible, 'Sell your possessions and give to the poor, and you will have treasure in heaven.' How are we to live if we give everything away?"

Julius smiled. "That verse does not suggest you give everything away. It doesn't even mean to sell your possessions in the way most people think. People think the verse means to sell your house, car, clothes and give that money to the poor. It doesn't.

"Sell your possessions means to get paid for the talents you possess and share. This is how we gain our livelihood, by selling our possessions, our talents, our skills, our passions. So, don't just give them away. Get paid for using your talents for the benefit of those who don't have them ... those are the poor we are talking about ... who may be rich in talents you don't possess.

"Of course, we can and should donate to the materially poor and enable them to develop and sell their possessions. That's what makes life worth living, the expression of self and the heart. It's a flow. That passage teaches us to increase the volume of our creative flow. It's like spiritual Viagra, although I prefer ginseng.

"When you know yourself, when you do what's really best for you, then you do what's best for everyone. It can be no other way. The trick is knowing what is really best for you. The sacred heart is not the suffering heart. Expression of possession is the path of the sacred heart. That is what gives you treasure in heaven, as that bible passage continues. That is how you 'Follow me,' as Christ said. And remember, you are already made in the image and likeness of God. It took the Church 300 years to confirm the divinity of Christ. Don't wait that long for yourself."

Richelieu leaned on his cane. He and Monsignor Tupelli listened from the shadows. "Good God!" Richelieu raspily whispered. "No wonder the man almost flunked theology in the seminary. What drivel." He looked to the cloudless sky. "Where's the lightning when you need it? When you expect it? How can he pontificate in such a way?"

Julius stood and smiled. "Thank you," he said, as he blessed the group.

As everyone in the crowd bowed their heads and crossed themselves, Tupelli spontaneously crossed himself. Richelieu elbowed him in the ribs.

Julius walked to one of the priests assisting him. "Luigi, I need a little peace and quiet and quality time." Julius made quotation mark signs with his fingers as he said, "I'll be in my "study" until it's time to practice."

"Yes, Your Holiness," the priest acknowledged.

Hours later Father Vincent, a young priest, hurried down a long, dark circular stairway. His black cassock fluttered behind him. As he descended, firelight began to play upon the brick walls. The sound of a hammer pounding steel echoed in the stairwell. The light got brighter and the sound louder.

Vincent came to the bottom of the stairs, then ran toward the light and sound. He entered an open area. A sign above it read "Papal Smithy." The priest saw Pope Julius and watched him for a moment.

A sweating Julius stood at a blacksmith forge and repaired the steel head of a halberd, the Vatican guards' traditional weapon. He wore his blacksmith apron, gloves, black pants and boots. Julius heated the halberd's head in the fire of the forge, pounded it on the anvil, and tempered it in the water bath.

Vincent finally interrupted. "Your Holiness, they are about to begin."

The pope continued to heat, beat and temper the steel.

The putti frequently fluttered around Julius in the smithy. They seemed to like it there.

"Should we tell him he has company?" the white putto innocently asked the red putto.

"Naw," the red putto said. "Remember what happened last time. Let's wait and see."

Julius stayed focused on his work. "I'm busy. Go," he snapped at the putti.

The putti scurried to a dark corner of the smithy.

Vincent called out louder, as he stood right behind Julius. "Your Holiness!"

Julius still did not hear him. Vincent tentatively touched Julius' shoulder and jumped back. Julius instantly brandished the halberd, pointed its hot red tip at Vincent's throat and stepped on the priest's foot, forcing him to the ground as the priest tried to step back.

Julius removed his earplugs and extended a hand to Vincent. "Oh, for Christ's sakes, Vincent. I'm sorry. I can't hear a thing with these earplugs in."

"It's fine, Your Holiness," Vincent said as Julius pulled him up. "Father Luigi warned me, but I had no idea you were so fast. Sorry to bother you. I was told to get you when the Swiss Guard's Drum & Bugle Corps started practice."

"Is it that late already?" Julius asked.

"Yes."

Julius quickly put the halberd against the wall. He stripped off his apron and gloves, and grabbed two other halberds he had already repaired. He ran up the stairs two at a time.

Coursing through the Apostolic Palace, Julius came to a room where sunlight streamed in from windows and an open balcony. He toweled off, then pulled on a clean beige shirt and black pants. Drums and bugles played outside.

"My favorite song," Julius said to himself.

He ran to the balcony, carrying the halberds. He looked into a courtyard. The dozen members of the Drum & Bugle Corps of the Swiss Vatican Guard marched below. The men wore their daily solid blue uniforms.

Leon, leader of the Drum & Bugle Corps, saw the pope on the balcony. He called to the troops.

"Halt!"

Julius grabbed a rope, rappelled into the courtyard and ran to the troops. Four guards had drums. Four had bugles. One played cymbals. Two marched along side Leon, without instruments.

"Here you go, Gregor, Nils. All fixed," Julius said as he tossed a halberd to each man next to Leon.

"Thank you, Your Holiness!" the men said together as they appraised the weapons.

Leon stepped forward and saluted the pope by placing his forearm across his chest.

"Your Holiness," he said.

"May I join you, Leon?" asked Julius.

"Of course, Your Holiness. We train only to serve you," Leon replied.

Leon motioned to a drummer. The drummer removed the drum and helped Julius into the drum strap, just as a black Mercedes pulled up.

Disappointed, Julius handed the drum back to Michael.

"Thank you, my son, but duty calls," Julius said.

Julius walked quickly to the car, but called over his shoulder. "Thank you, Leon. See you tomorrow on the firing range. *Ciao!*"

Leon saluted again. "*Jawohl*, Holy Father. Tomorrow."

Julius slid into the Mercedes. "Hello, monsignor," he said.

The bespectacled Monsignor Tupelli answered Julius softly and breathlessly. "Your Holiness, Cardinal Richelieu is concerned that your upcoming trip to Caracas poses great danger to you. He requests an audience with you as soon as possible."

Julius turned to the effeminate monsignor in disbelief. "That's what you want to talk about? Now? Judas Priest. Richelieu is a candy ass. What would he do if the world were truly dangerous?" Julius asked.

Julius' smile actually left his face. He paused thoughtfully as he looked out the window of the car. He turned to the monsignor.

"Tell Richelieu to forget Caracas," he said, then added emphatically, "What you and I need to talk about are the Julius II Games!"

Tupelli sighed. "Very well. I met with the committee earlier today, Your Holiness. Everything seems ready."

"Excellent," Julius acknowledged. "I'm going to the training arena soon to practice. What about tonight?"

"Your mother has a wonderful banquet planned for the contestants," Tupelli replied.

"I'm not surprised. She's an angel. And tomorrow? There's no hiccup with the coverage?"

"No. The cable network agreed to our requested changes. The broadcast of the Games will start at 10 a.m., as planned," answered Tupelli.

Julius' eyes glossed over. "Julius II, now he was a Pope for the Ages" he said. "If we ever come up with a Patron Saint of Popes, it would have to be Julius."

"We have a Patron Saint of Popes, Your Holiness," the monsignor corrected. "It's Peter."

"He'd be my next choice," Julius agreed as he glanced at his watch. "Damn. I'm late for a meeting." He tapped the driver on the shoulder. "Giles, can you drop me off at the practice arena, please?"

"Yes, Your Eminence." Julius sniffed the air out of the open car window. "My god. Is my mother making pierogis? I better have a little snack first. Giles, take the monsignor to his office. Then come back here, please."

"Of course, Your Eminence," Giles said.

Julius got out of the car.

"But Your Holiness," Tupelli protested, "we need to finalize the theme of your sermon for Sunday so we can promote ..."

Julius talked and laughed over one shoulder then the other as he walked quickly toward the back door of the Vatican Kitchen. "Monsignor, I'm the Pope, the Caped Crusader, Zorro of Zion, Successor of St. Peter, Captain of the Clergy, *Pontificus Maximus*, Bodyguard to God, Six-sixty-six."

Julius stopped to face Tupelli, who was still in the car. "The people will show up whether or not I know what I'll talk about," he said. "Besides, words never got anyone into Heaven, although I'm not sure we can say the same about Hell."

Julius scurried off.

The monsignor raised his hand as if to speak, but slumped back into the seat in despair. "Prayer, Your Holiness. Prayer," he said breathlessly to himself. "We need prayer, not pierogis."

The Mercedes rolled out of the courtyard.

Chapter VI

The Tiara of Julius II

A GUIDE SPOKE to a group of tourists in the Vatican Museums. They stood by a glass display case. Inside of it was a large conical shaped tiara made of silver. It stood over forty-five centimeters, or eighteen inches, high.

"Here is the Tiara of Pope Julius II," the guide explained. "Known as 'Heaven's Crown,' it is adorned with pearls, rubies, diamonds and topped with The Crucifix Moonstone, the world's largest emerald."

"Jesus!" a tourist exclaimed.

An old woman turned and looked scornfully at him.

The guide continued. "The tiara was shaped in felt and overlaid with a silver mesh. Its three separate bands were screwed together over the mesh and inlaid with jewels. It is valued at €20,000,000 or over $25,000,000.

"Julius II created the Swiss Vatican Guards in 1506," the guide continued. "When Rome was sacked in 1527 by soldiers of King Charles V of Spain, Pope Clement only escaped due to the bravery of his small force of Vatican guards, almost all of whom were killed during the attack. The few left alive stashed the pope at *Castel Sant'Angelo,* the Castle of the Holy Angel, which is only a few hundred meters from here on the Tiber River. From there, Pope Clement used this tiara to pay a ransom. It was lost for years, but finally returned to the Vatican.

"When Napoleon came to power after the French Revolution, he was determined to control the papacy, as the Church had temporarily fallen out of favor with the French," the guide explained. "So he imprisoned Pope Pius VI, who died shortly afterward. When Pope Pius VII resisted Napoleon, Napoleon personally imprisoned Pope Pius VII in a palace in Avignon, France, locking the door himself.

"To endear himself to the French, humiliate the papacy and help pay for his wars, Napoleon looted the Vatican again in 1809. Thousands of items were displayed in the Louvre, which was temporarily named *Musee' Napoleon.*

"But Napoleon's real ambition was to secure this tiara," the guide pointed to the display case again, "and use it to crown himself pope. It never happened. Vatican guards hid it in a convent. Steeped in mystery and prophecy, legend has it that the tiara can only be worn by someone worthy of its splendor. The Mother Superior charged with its safekeeping was ostensibly killed when trying to put it on her own head.

"After Napoleon's final defeat in 1814, most Vatican treasure, including the tiara, was returned to the Papacy. It took three years and thousands of wagonloads to cart all the treasure back to the Vatican.

"The tiara has been under heavy guard ever since, and will be tomorrow when on display at the Julius II Games."

The guide led the crowd to another glass display and said, "Here we have the foreskin of St. Peter the Great ..."

Chapter VII

Pregame

THE MERCEDES PULLED up to the Julius II Games' stadium, where participants were practicing. Julius V put down a plate with a pierogi on it and licked his fingers. He grabbed his recurve bow and quiver of arrows, got out, and walked toward Sarge, who had been finalizing security. The two men smiled and embraced in a manly, shoulder slapping way.

"How go the preparations, my friend?" asked Julius.

"Excellent, Your Holiness. We have nothing short of the Angel of Death at each entrance to assure that all goes well," Sarge replied confidently. "There will be nothing in or out that we don't want in or out."

The men strolled about the ground. Julius II Games' contestants practiced track, field, wrestling and strength events. Mayans in headdresses, multi-colored body paint and red loincloths played basketball.

"Remind me," said Julius. "How many teams are entered this year?"

"More than ever," Sarge replied. "One hundred fourteen teams and nearly six hundred competitors."

"There's excitement in the air!" Julius said, as he suddenly caught a basketball that flew out of play. It looked like a human skull. He tossed it back to one of the Mayan who went in for an alley-oop dunk.

"Great to see the Mayans here after that 2012 debacle," Julius commented. "How'd they handle us nixing their request for human sacrifice?"

"They almost walked out," Sarge answered, "but we told them they could use the Vatican Observatory to help them with their next calendar."

An Amish horse buggy equipped with knife blades on the wheels, made famous in the movie, Ben-Hur, trundled by. It sported an orange slow-vehicle triangle on the back. The men waved to each other.

"I assume the Amish are prohibitive favorites in the chariot race," Julius observed.

"Yep," Sarge confirmed. "We let them keep their wheel blades so they'd help build the bleachers."

"Good call."

A heavy aluminum keg spiraled over a wall. Julius pushed Sarge out of the way as it flew toward his head. The keg hit the ground with a thump and bounced to a stop.

Niklas, a powerfully built young man in Vatican blue T-shirt and shorts, ran around from behind the wall.

"For God's sakes, Niklas, what's going on?" Sarge was livid.

"Sorry, milords. I was practicing the keg toss for the strong man contest. This one got away from me," Niklas said.

"But the Julius Games are only for clergy. You are a Vatican guard," Sarge reminded him.

Julius stepped in. "I made Niklas a deacon, so he's clergy now. The Protestants handed us our asses in the strength events during the last games, so I brought Niklas in."

"As a ringer," Sarge accused.

"No, as a deacon. In fact, Niklas will help distribute Holy Communion at Mass before the Games," Julius explained.

"The Lutherans may start another Reformation over this," Sarge commented.

Julius was unperturbed. "Doubtful. Remember that Viking they brought in from St. Olaf's? Claimed he was a shaman, but more like a sham. The Lutherans won't pull out. They can't afford their own games, so they want to beat us at our own."

Julius rolled the keg back to Niklas with his foot.

"Thank you, Your Holiness," Niklas said, shouldered the keg and trotted off.

As Julius and Sarge watched Niklas disappear around the wall, they noticed a woman running the hurdles on the track well over a hundred meters away. She cruised at unbelievable speed. Her medium brown spandex shorts and white tank top cradled her feline-like, athletic body.

"My god," Julius drawled. "What team is she on?"

"Ours," answered Sarge. "She's all nun."

"A nun. Really? As in Catholic nun?" Julius asked.

"Yes."

The nun cruised smoothly around a turn. From that new angle the men could see her firm butt and legs.

"Those legs work, I mean the Lord works in mysterious ways," Julius observed. "Who is she? Sister Mary Cheetah?"

"Sister LaTrelle Terre, a French nun from the order of Sainte Jeanne d'Arc. She's on the Frenchies' parkour team."

"LaTrelle?"

After the last hurdle, the woman did a triple jump and ended in a flip. Julius shook his head slowly as he watched her.

"I knew a LaTrelle years ago. I pray she is not the same one."

The woman walked off the track, grabbed a towel and patted herself and her shoulder-length hair dry.

Julius turned from the nun and back to Sarge. "I'm going to take Eli for a few turns around the arena and ride him back to the Vatican," he said. "He's saddled and ready to go."

"Yes, Your Holiness. Will I see you at the athletes' banquet tonight?"

"I'm afraid not," Julius answered. "Tonight's my poker game. I need to make extra cash to pay for the food. My mom will MC the banquet."

The men parted and Julius walked into the lavish and well-kept horse barn. He acknowledged several stable hands who tended horses, then Julius whistled.

Eli's ears perked up. Then he released the stall door with his mouth and trotted down the stable alleyway toward Julius. Other horses neighed deferentially.

Julius affectionately rubbed Eli's head as Eli rubbed against Julius' arm. Then Julius swung up on Eli, trotted down the alleyway and outside into the arena set up for horseback archery.

With a quiver of arrows on his back and half dozen arrows in his bow hand, Julius quickly and accurately impaled target after target with arrows, as Eli cantered inside the arena. A groom came out and tossed small, round targets into the air. Others were released from a throwing device. Julius hit every one.

After about twenty minutes, Julius said, "We're there, Eli. Let's go home. I need you at your best tomorrow for the start of the Games."

Eli pinned his ears back, raced out of the arena and into the sunset. Dirt flew from his hooves. The putti flew hard, but could not keep up.

A dark blue banner with large white lettering hung on the wall by the dinner buffet. It read 'Welcome to the 2nd Julius II Games.'

Several hundred athletes milled around the banquet hall. They represented religious and spiritual sects from throughout the world. Most were dressed in traditional garb. Some were seated at round dining tables; some were in the double buffet line.

Two athletes, a Catholic priest in his mid-thirties and a thirty year old black witch doctor, stood on opposite sides of the buffet line. Both skewered the same piece of chicken. Neither let it go. The witch doctor shook his baboon head rattle at the priest. His eyes bugged out.

"Let go, Black Robe," the witch doctor threatened, "or my next rattle will be your head."

The priest bugged out his eyes. He whipped out a large crucifix, and held it almost against the witch doctor's forehead.

"Hyena scum!" he said. "You'll burn in hell even hotter with my crucifix up your ass."

The two men levitated and circled each other in the air over the crowd, cursing each other. A wild, carnival atmosphere ensued. Pieces of chicken rose up from the pan. Cheering, jeering, raucous spectators urged them on. They began to place bets. A rabbi held the money.

"Maggot!" the priest spat.

"Faggot!" countered the witch doctor.

They held each other by the shoulders as a bleating goat, food, chairs, bottles of wine, plates and other serving items flew around them. A woman in a veil was in trance, swaying.

"Stop right there!"

Everything and everyone froze. Teeny Sister Lorraine stood directly underneath the two men and looked up at them.

"Jesus, it's the pope's mom," someone in the crowd said.

"Come down right now," Lorraine ordered.

Both men looked at each other sheepishly and slowly descended. Everything else fell to the floor. The nun grabbed both of them by an ear. They squealed and twisted, but could not get away. She glared at the priest.

"Give me that crucifix," she said and held out a hand.

The priest complied.

She turned to the witch doctor and said, "Give me that rattle."

He did.

She looked back at the priest. "What's your name?"

"Father Ted O'Connor, sister."

She turned to the black man. "And you?"

He mumbled something incoherently. The nun twisted his ear again. He squealed loudly and squirmed.

"Reverend George Peal!" he bellowed with an English accent.

Lorraine glared at the witch doctor. "Wait here," she said.

She hustled the priest to a corner and jammed his face in it. "Stay here until I come back for you," she commanded.

She stormed over to the witch doctor, who stood dejected and timid. She grabbed and twisted his ear again.

"Ow! Ow! Ow! Ow! Ow! Ow! Ow!" he protested.

Lorraine ushered him into an opposite corner of the room and jammed his face in it. "And you stay here until I come back for you!" she commanded.

Then Lorraine addressed the crowd. She held the crucifix and rattle in one hand and tapped her other palm with them.

"Anyone else want to fight over my sisters' cooking?"

No one said a word.

"I didn't think so. Now, no more talking until everyone is done eating. We're shorthanded, so if any one of you bozos utters a word, I'll pull you out of the Games and into the kitchen," she warned.

Many athletes sat back down. Others got back in the buffet line, except for the priest and witch doctor. All was quiet, except for sound of silverware scraping plates.

Chapter VIII

Let the Games Begin!

THE NEXT MORNING, athletes began to arrive at the Games arena shortly after sunrise. Some were in ceremonial dress; others in competitive uniforms. A bustle of activity came from radio and news crews from around the world setting up media stations. Vatican guards and other uniformed and plainclothes officers checked all incoming utility vehicles and personnel for proper identification. Security had been tight, both seen and unseen, especially in the last week leading up to the games. With events scheduled to start at mid-morning, spectators began to arrive by eight a.m.

The Vatican had again contracted with PAGAN – the Pro/Am Games Analysis Network – for television coverage. The network's top sports analysts, Lisa and Neil, took their seats at the announcers' table, positioned between the center of the grandstand and the running track. They did one last sound check with the production crew. Lisa looked quite robust in her lavender blouse, gray blazer and matching pants. Neil was sharply dressed with a silver shirt, fuchsia patterned tie and dark blue suit.

The day was cloudy. Fog had rolled in from the Mediterranean. Lisa was fluffing her hair when Neil got the 3-2-1 count down to begin.

"Good morning and welcome to Rome's Olympiad Arena," said an ebullient Neil. "Today marks the opening day of the Pope Julius II Vatican Games. Held every four years, this four-day event features religious and spiritual athletes from throughout the world."

Lisa followed her cue. "Exactly, Neil. And these athletes are all ready to 'Go for the Gold,' so to speak."

"And some are extremely gifted," Neil added. "Several foolishly gave up big contracts to do the Lord's – or whoever's – work."

"Maybe that's what Christ meant when he said, 'The poor will always be with you,'" Lisa said.

"They will be if you turn down the big money," Neil concluded.

The Vatican Drum & Bugle Corps marched in front of the announcers' table. The cameras focused on them, as Lisa added commentary.

"The Vatican Guards' Drum & Bugle Corps is adding to the pageantry," she said.

"Many tourists think the guards are just for show," Neil explained off camera, "but they can slit your throat faster than you can say Jesus, Mary and Joseph. Beneath each candy-striped uniform is a lean, mean fighting machine."

The cameras switched back to the announcers.

"Not to mention a 9mm Heckler & Koch MP5 submachine gun," Lisa added.

Neil looked at Lisa in disbelief, "Really?" he asked.

"Really," she answered.

"Good to know." Neil cast his eyes briefly around the arena. "The crowd is obviously pumped to get this party started. Where do we begin?"

"Today's featured highlight will be the parkour competition," Lisa explained, "one of several co-ed events. Each team prepares according to tradition."

Cameras panned first to the Rastafarians, who sat on green, yellow and red blankets in the grass. Wearing similar colored shorts and t-shirts, they dreadlocked each others' hair, smoked huge doobies and listened to reggae. Neil and Lisa commented off camera.

"Jamaica's Rastafarians are obviously feeling it," Neil observed.

"Or not feeling it," Lisa suggested.

A camera cut to the Druids. They were building a miniature Stonehenge through rock levitation.

"Team Druid is rocking out," Neil observed.

"Great people to have around for any building project," Lisa affirmed.

Next the cameras focused on the Shaolin monks' warmup area. Four monks took turns being kicked in the groin.

"China's Shaolin monks are demonstrating the revered Iron Crotch Technique," Neil explained.

"If that's a form of birth control, I'm surprised the Vatican allows it," Lisa commented.

Finally, the cameras revealed the most popular parkour team, the four nuns from the St. Jeanne d'Arc convent in France's Alsace Province. Sisters LaTrelle, Susan, Angela and Carmel were tied to stakes above a funeral pyre. Flames lapped the wood. Each nun wore a brown, ankle-length peasant dress. Each nun was gorgeous.

Neil added his commentary. "The Sisters de Jeanne d'Arc are the only all-nun team to participate in these games."

"They certainly give new meaning to the term 'warming up,'" Lisa commented.

The ropes that tied the nuns burned and broke. One by one, each nun back flipped out of the fire and into a huge frying pan. The crowd cheered wildly. Each nun genuflected, crossed herself and trotted off.

Neil stated the obvious. "Out of the fire and into the frying pan."

"Well said," Lisa smiled in support. "Oh, there's Pope Julius V. These Games are his brainchild, but he was expelled from them four years ago when he was Father Jules Sole'."

Neil acknowledged the pope's presence. "Yes, his last name is Italian for Sun."

"He certainly brings a sunny countenance to everything," Lisa added.

Lisa pulled out a mirror and checked her look.

Julius rode Eli in the infield near the grandstand. His bow was in a scabbard and his quiver was on his back.

Lisa fluffed her hair again and added blush and lipstick as she said, "The story we have is that his father, Pope Damiano, had fixed the horseback archery competition so an underdog would win. Father Jules refused to go along and won the competition."

Julius smiled, waved and shook hands with spectators across the low barricade that separated them from the athletes.

Neil picked up on Lisa's explanation. "Father Jules' win cost his father a lot of money, as he had bet on the underdog."

As Julius rode by, young women screamed and jumped up and down, as if they were at a rock concert.

"To punish him, the pope exiled his son to Montana, took away his horse and all of his archery equipment, with the fiat that Father Jules could never compete in these Games again," Lisa said, as she smoothed her lipstick with a pinky finger.

Julius smiled and blessed the cheering crowd with the sign of the cross.

"Well, as Julius V, he's sitting pretty now," Neil observed.

"And he looks every inch 'The Warrior Pope,' although he downplays that image and attributes it only to Julius II," Lisa said, as she snapped her makeup kit closed.

Julius flashed the peace sign. Eli pranced.

"Yes, he's quite the horseman, archer and swordsman," Neil agreed.

"And showman," Lisa affirmed.

"And holy man," Neil added.

"So shaman or showman, eh?" Lisa smiled as she asked.

"Televangelist?" Neil suggested.

"He'd make a fortune," Lisa pronounced.

"He's doing pretty well as pope," Neil said.

Lisa stood up as she said, "Let's see if we can get this most popular and public of popes here to talk.

"Your Holiness? Your Holiness?" Lisa called as she waved.

Julius rode to the announcers' table and greeted the two commentators.

"Good morning, Lisa. Neil. Great to see you again."

"And you, Your Holiness," Lisa said.

Neil leaned in to get Julius' attention. "Your Holiness, people from all faiths and beliefs are at these Games. What are you trying to accomplish by hosting them?"

"To show that nothing says competition like religion," Julius deadpanned.

Lisa looked at him stunned. "You can't be serious," she said.

Julius' smile returned and he laughed. "Actually, these Games prove that God doesn't play favorites, no matter how many times we cross ourselves or cross others. As a matter of fact, God's not playing at all. But we are. That's the purpose of the Julius II Games. To play."

"And who was Pope Julius II?" Neil asked, trying to steer the conversation.

Julius' eyes practically glossed over. "The greatest pope ever," he replied. "Never in history were war, art, indulgences – some would say extortion – and Catholicism so intertwined or revered as under Julius II. These games are dedicated to that man and his ideals."

"And what can you tell us about this magnificent tiara?" Lisa asked, pointing to the Tiara of Julius II.

The tiara was behind the announcers in a glass case on a pedestal. Four armed Vatican guards surrounded the case.

"It is the crowning achievement of Julius II's legacy," Julius answered. "It doesn't just embody excess, which it does. It also represents the highest ideals of male and female, positive and negative. Think of it as the fulcrum of, the nexus between, heaven and earth."

"Why such importance?" Lisa asked.

Julius smiled at her again. "You've heard of as above so below?" he asked.

Lisa blushed, hoping that was a sexual innuendo, "Of course."

"Some believe Julius II precisely placed the tiara's top jewels to help create heaven on earth. But in the wrong hands or on the wrong head, the reverse can happen. It could make hell on earth or earth in heaven; difficult to say which would be worse."

Lisa tossed her head and laughed. "Such a joker!"

Neil impatiently interrupted. "You are favored again in the archery events, Your Holiness. How do you think you'll do?"

Julius looked at Neil. "If God played favorites, I wouldn't have a chance. But as long as I have Eli, I'll do fine."

"He's magnificent," Lisa chimed.

Eli enthusiastically nodded his head, as the pope patted him.

"Yes, he is," Julius acknowledged.

"What's his story?" Neil asked.

"Eli was a four year old when I won him nearly three years ago in a game of Russian Roulette from a Russian colonel. Eli was one stall away from being ground up for sausage. He and the Russian may have traded places after the Russian lost."

Eli stomped and snorted. Julius glanced around the stadium.

"I better go," Julius said as he shook hands with Lisa and Neil. "It's time to start."

Lisa looked to the camera and gave it a big smile. "Let the games begin!" she cheered.

Neil rolled his eyes.

The camera focused on the starting line of the parkour race. The eight teams had begun to line up. In addition to the Rastas, Druids, Shaolin monks and Catholic nuns, they included a co-ed team of Lakota, a team of Australian aborigines, a Muslim-Christian team from Nigeria and a group of rabbis. The Sisters de Jeanne d'Arc stepped out of their peasant dresses

56

and revealed soft suede brown shorts and white jerseys. Members of each men's team did an approving double take.

"This promises to be a great event," Lisa said. "Although parkour's origins are non-competitive, it is included in the Julius Games for the pure beauty and camaraderie of the sport."

"Each team needs to collect four flags, the furthest one is about a mile from the stadium," Neil added, "and they are in difficult and high locations about Rome."

Pre-positioned television cameras showed the eight team flags atop the four locations: the spiky tower of Piazza del Gesu, the Villa Borghese, the steeple atop St. Ignatius Church and the rooftop angel of the Castel Sant'Angelo on the banks of the Tiber River.

"The first team to collect all four of their flags and cross the finish line here in the stadium wins," said Lisa.

"And in parkour, there is no route," Neil added.

"And there are no rules. Athletes simply go from Point A to any Point B anyway they can: running, jumping, flipping, climbing," added Lisa.

Neil gave an update. "The teams are at the starting line. We anticipate them splitting up and sending a runner to each of the four sites."

"And our cameras will track this fast paced action," said Lisa.

The starting gun fired. The athletes ran together and out of the arena, where they split up. The crowd cheered.

Suddenly, Sister Angela from the Jeanne d'Arc parkour team sprang on and over the announcers' table.

Lisa ducked. "What the hell?"

Sister Angela flipped toward the Vatican guards guarding the tiara. She landed on the shoulders of one of them, touched two guards lightly on the face and smiled.

Carmela bounded onto the announcers' table. She did a handspring over Lisa and Neil and landed on another guard's shoulders. The guards looked up at her admiringly. Two fast moving Amish buggies scurried in front of the announcers' table. The knife blades on their wheels twirled menacingly, then slashed the legs of the tiara's pedestal. The tiara teetered.

Angela jumped off the shoulders of the guard toward Carmela. Carmela flipped her high into the air. Angela caught the tiara as it fell. She hit the ground running.

The buggies circled back to the nuns. Angela jumped into one. Carmela twisted off the guard's shoulders and into the other. The buggies tore away down the track. Two guards aimed their MP5s and prepared to fire.

"Halt!" Sarge hollered to his men. "You may hit the tiara!"

The men lowered their weapons.

From over a hundred meters away, Julius saw the theft. He stopped greeting the grandstand crowd and immediately galloped Eli toward the nuns.

The buggies raced out of the arena onto the crowded and foggy streets of Rome. The blades in their wheels spun ominously. Julius rode hard in pursuit. He and Eli quickly disappeared through the arena's main gate.

A shaken Lisa exclaimed, "My god! The Sisters de Jeanne d'Arc just stole the Tiara of Julius II."

Neil adjusted his coat and looked at the camera. "This crowd is shocked. I'm shocked. The Vatican guards appear to be shocked and the pope just rode out of here without any security."

"Whether this is real or not, it should help the ratings," Lisa adlibbed.

Two Amish men clothed only in long underwear and hats ran out of a tunnel and onto the track, pointing to the buggies. They shook off the last of the ropes that wrapped their arms. Two Vatican guards on motorcycles gave chase. They raced out of the arena, with back tires throwing dirt on the Amish men, who kicked the air and threw their hats to the ground.

Sisters LaTrelle and Susan raced the buggies side by side through the crowded, foggy streets of Rome. Julius worked Eli through the traffic, barely gaining on the nuns when the Vatican guards on motorcycles caught up to him. At that moment, the buggies split up at a circular street that went around a fountain.

"Get the one on the right!" Julius ordered.

The guards nodded. They followed the buggy as it wove among cars, trucks and busses. The buggy hopped a sidewalk, went down a narrow alley, then back to a street, barely missing the front of a truck. It jumped a curb into a park, then went up a hill. Its wheel blade pruned a hedge for a grateful worker. He waved and smiled at the sisters.

The motorcycles went around the park, then zigzagged through pedestrians on the sidewalk as it sped toward the nuns approaching the hilltop. One almost intercepted the buggy, but had to dodge the wheel blades. After the driver regained control of his bike, both motorcycles closed in behind the nuns.

The buggy raced through trees toward a crowd at a wedding reception. Guests jumped out of its way as it hurled toward the bride and groom embraced in their first dance. One of the buggy's blades wrapped around the bride's wedding dress. It spun her around and tore off her gown, stripping her to her bra, panties and stockings. The dress flew up in the face of both motorcycle drivers. They crashed into each other.

"Damn it," one of the guards lamented, as he got his bike off the ground.

"Jesus Christ!" the other said, as he looked behind them.

The Father of the Bride, and the rest of her Sicilian family, stormed toward the two men. The men got their bikes going just before the mob caught up with them. They took off after the nuns again.

The buggy raced through the streets amidst honking traffic and running pedestrians with the motorcycles in pursuit. From the opposite direction came police cars and sirens, chasing a get-away car from a bank robbery. As the get-away car raced toward the buggy, the buggy deftly coursed to its right, slashing the car's tires. The car crashed into a fountain. Police immediately surrounded the robbers.

The buggy and bikes blasted into the arena of the Mausoleum of Augustus, preserved as an attraction from the days of the Roman Emperors. Racing around the arena like modern charioteers, the guards attempted to squeeze the buggy to a stop, but Sister Susan skillfully worked the wheel blades into the spokes of a motorcycle, ripping the back wheel. The bike crashed into the wall; the driver somersaulted into the dirt. The other guard circled back to rescue his friend, who painfully got on the motorcycle behind the driver. They watched the buggy disappear under an archway and back onto the street.

Careening through traffic and shoppers, the buggy headed toward a Metro rail station, with the guards in pursuit. People jumped out of the way as the horse blasted through the turnstile. Wheel blades slashed the ticket dispenser and the buggy squeaked by. The motorcycle raced through the turnstile and closed in.

Sisters Susan and Angela rode into a train as it opened its doors. The horse got through, but the wheels struck and stuck on the doorframes. The nuns jumped out of the buggy, ran to and through the open train door on the other side and got into another train.

With the doors blocked by the horse and buggy, the guards jumped off the motorcycle. They squeezed past the horse and buggy as a train left the station. The guards looked up in time to see the nuns smiling sweetly at them as they waved good-bye through a window. The guards politely, but unhappily, waved back.

Meanwhile, Julius and Eli chased the second buggy through fog and traffic into a cemetery. As the buggy raced past a gravesite, Julius reined up when mourners at a funeral recognized him.

"Pope Julius!" exclaimed the priest, as he prayed over the casket.

Julius got off Eli to bless them and comfort the widow and family. In a gesture of appreciation, a woman wiped his face with her white scarf. When she saw the image of Julius' face on her scarf, she fell to her knees and wept effusively.

Julius helped her up, wiped her tears and then mounted Eli. Eli reared and galloped out of the cemetery. Julius rode up the hill in an adjacent park, scanning for the buggy. Finally he saw it stuck in traffic on an overpass partially covered by fog. Julius urged Eli forward. He worked Eli through traffic, galloped up a ramp and caught up to the buggy. He grabbed the horse's reins, only to see a stunned elderly Amish couple sitting beneath the buggy's canopy.

"Sorry, folks. Wrong buggy," Julius said apologetically.

"Are you filming a spaghetti western?" asked the Amish man.

"Do they still make those?" Julius asked in return.

"I don't know," cooed the Amish woman, as she squeezed her husband's arm. "We're a little behind the times."

Julius gazed around and saw another Amish buggy stopped at a light on a lower street near the Tiber River. He lightly put his heels into Eli's sides. Eli immediately responded and galloped through vehicular and pedestrian traffic. Julius and Eli closed in on the buggy as it bounced down a stairway into the catacombs of Rome.

The buggy sped by an archaeological site where several archaeologists worked by lantern light. One of its razor wheels cut through a clay wall. Hundreds of skeletons fell out and spilled onto the workers. Eli ran through the bones. The buggy flew up a ramp and onto the streets. It turned hard down a narrow alley. Its wheel blades almost touched the walls. Julius and Eli closed in. A delivery truck blocked the far end of the alley.

LaTrelle passed the reins to Carmela, grabbed a fire escape landing, and swung backward out of the buggy. She flipped over Julius and Eli, landed on the grounds and ran back toward the street behind them.

"Nimble wench," Julius said as he backed Eli out of the alley.

Carrying the tiara in a backpack, LaTrelle raced down the street against traffic. She jumped on cars and disappeared in the street.

Julius stood in his stirrups, but could not see her. He gazed around as Eli trotted along the Tiber River. The fog and traffic were thick; the sounds of the city were loud. Then Julius heard a helicopter in the cloudy skies.

"Castel Sant'Angelo," he said to himself.

Julius rode hard, weaving through the traffic to get to Castel Sant'Angelo. He heard the helicopter getting closer. As he approached the massive Castel Sant'Angelo, he saw LaTrelle scaling its outer wall like a spider. Tourists jumped out of their way as he galloped to the Castel, plunged Eli through a main doorway and rode Eli up the Castel's stairs toward the roof.

Outside, LaTrelle pulled herself to the roof and ran to the angel at its center.

The helicopter was overhead, somewhat blurred in the fog, but a hand partially tucked inside a shirt could be seen painted on its side. The helicopter lowered a cable.

Julius and Eli exploded through the roof's door as LaTrelle pulled up her team's parkour flag from the Castel's angel, stuffed it in a rear pocket, hooked her belt to a cable harness and signaled the helicopter to lift her.

People touring the Castel watched her.

A woman pointed at LaTrelle and exclaimed, "It's the Virgin Mary!"

"She's ascending into heaven!" a man hollered as he crossed himself.

Some people bowed, others knelt, in prayer and silence.

"My god, these Christians are a superstitious lot," Julius said, nocking an arrow on his bowstring. As he rode, he aimed at LaTrelle, who was in the air and over seventy-five meters away.

"The pope is going to shoot the Mother of God!" a tourist cried out.

"I heard he would do such a thing!" proclaimed another.

Julius let an arrow fly. It cut one of the shoulder straps of the backpack holding the tiara.

LaTrelle's eyes opened wide in surprise. "*Mon Dieu!*" she exclaimed.

Julius shot another arrow. It cut the backpack's other shoulder strap.

LaTrelle held on to the pack with one hand. *"Incroyable!"* she exclaimed.

Julius nocked another arrow as he rode almost under LaTrelle. He leaned back in the saddle and shot.

LaTrelle tossed the backpack into the helicopter as the third arrow nipped her butt. It cut a piece of fabric off her shorts, impaled her parkour flag and lifted it from her pocket. LaTrelle scurried into the helicopter. As she looked down to see torn pink lace panties through the tear, her eyes met Julius'. He steadied Eli and returned her look. She scowled and gave him the *bras d'honneur,* slapping her bicep so her arm flew up. It was the French equivalent to the finger.

The helicopter flew off, whipping around the arrow with the flag. It fell toward Julius. He snatched it out of the air. He half-heartedly obliged the few tourists who asked for his blessing. Then, emotionless, he turned Eli and rode away.

Chapter IX

Fellowship of the Tiara

"I TAKE FULL responsibility, Your Holiness," Sarge said to Julius as they walked out of Eli's stall.

"No one could have foreseen this, Sarge, and you can't very well shoot a nun in the back."

"But..."

Julius smiled. "Get ready to travel. I need you."

A short time later, Julius brusquely entered the super secret Papal Peace Center, the Vatican's equivalent to a "war room," except designed to make love not war. Papal staff monitored rows of computer screens that displayed events from around the world. Julius walked up to Kurt, the Vatican Guard room commander.

"Can you pick up the tiara, Kurt?" Julius asked.

"No, Your Holiness. We had it for a moment over the city, but then the helicopter disappeared. It must have some sort of cloaking device."

"Can we get help from Scotland Yard? The C.I.A? NATO? Interpol? Mossad?"

"Mossad? Really?" Kurt asked.

Julius shrugged. "Maybe not. But with over a billion Catholics on the planet we must know someone who knows something." Julius thoughtfully looked at a monitor, then asked. "How soon can you get the Council of the Reserve Guard together?"

"You don't mean?"

"I do," Julius responded. "This is that big."

"Twenty four hours."

"Eighteen?" Julius pushed.

Kurt thought for a moment. "Eighteen, yes, we can do that."

"Tell them we'll meet at Chateau de Ranged tomorrow at 6 a.m."

"Will you cancel The Games?" Kurt asked.

"No. I won't let whoever stole the tiara steal the Games, too."

"But, Holiness," Kurt responded, "les Sisters de Jeanne D'Arc stole the tiara."

"The nuns are puppets," Julius said derisively. "I want the mastermind. Besides, no one at their convent returned my call."

Julius tromped away.

Cardinal Richelieu leaned his gnarled old body on his cane. His thin, greasy hair shone beneath the red silk skullcap. He and Monsignor Tupelli watched from the shadows as Julius walked briskly from the Papal Peace Center.

"I'm still amazed. How could the bastard son of an Italian pope and an American nun become head of the Catholic Church?" Richelieu asked rhetorically.

"The cardinals elected him," Tupelli answered.

"Not all of the cardinals," Richelieu said indignantly.

"Not all of the cardinals know this time of prophecy would come," was Tupelli's cryptic reply.

"Julius didn't; but now that he's pope, I don't know what he knows."

"Less than he thinks," Tupelli said.

Richelieu confronted Tupelli. "You said he was elected to prevent the tiara from being stolen."

"And I said he was elected to get it back if it ever was," Tupelli replied. Richelieu shook his head.

"It's a mystery."

"It's a prophecy," Tupelli corrected.

"Julius is a problem," Richelieu said flatly.

"Losing the tiara is a bigger problem," countered Tupelli.

Richelieu seemed to talk to himself. "The damage he could do to the Church."

"He's too busy with fun and games to make changes," Tupelli comforted.

"And to think we need him now to get the tiara back," Richelieu spat.

"Then don't think about it," Tupelli counseled.

"But if he does, he'll be more popular than ever … unless we crucify him some way," Richelieu said wickedly.

The cardinal diabolically rubbed his hands together, but clumsily slipped from his cane and fell to the ground.

Tupelli lifted him up. "Martyrdom makes heroes more beloved."

"A sex scandal then," Richelieu said as he brushed dirt from a palm.

"One more won't make an impact," Tupelli said.

"And to think he could be pope for another thirty years," Richelieu observed lividly.

"Then don't think about it," Tupelli counseled again.

"I prefer an Irishman over that mongrel," Richelieu growled.

Julius hustled around a corner. The two men stepped slightly out of the shadows to watch him.

"Where he's off to now? The gym?" Richelieu asked.

"A cocktail party?" Tupelli offered.

"The horse track?" Richelieu knew Julius' habits well.

"A Formula One race?" Tupelli wondered.

"The country club?"

Julius unlocked and opened a door to a small, private Vatican chapel. He walked in.

The other two men look at each other incredulously. "A chapel?" they asked each other.

Soft light illuminated the modest chapel. Julius crossed himself at the holy water fountain. He deliberately walked up the chapel's short and narrow main aisle. He stopped at a Renaissance-era painting on the wall to one side of the altar.

The title of the painting was "The Crucifixion of St. Peter the Apostle." It featured an almost naked and bearded old man being crucified upside down. A hostile, jeering crowd surrounded him. Several putti were in the scene.

Julius put his back to the painting, bent down and put his head between his knees to make better eye contact with the man on the cross in the painting.

"Hello, Peter," Julius said. "We seldom see eye to eye, but we need to talk. When that myth started that you were crucified upside down, almost everything else righteous and true in the Catholic Church got turned on its head. Things haven't been the same since." Julius stood up straight and turned to speak to the painting. He looked down into the crucified man's eyes.

"It's going to take more than a few proper crucifixions to set things straight," Julius said, "but that's what I intend to do now, beginning with who stole the tiara."

Julius turned to leave, then stopped. He faced the painting.

"Any help will be appreciated," he added.

The red and white putti flew out of the painting. They lagged behind Julius as he walked down the aisle to the door. Their little butts conspicuously puckered and swayed beneath their wings as they high-fived each other.

"Woo-hoo! Crucifixion is back on the table!" the red putto joyfully exclaimed.

"Theologian and Executioner, I love this guy!" the white putto praised.

"I pity the poor devil with the tiara," the red putto said happily.

"I pray life will not become hell on earth for the rest of us," the white putto said a bit thoughtfully.

"Then I pray Julius is more brain than brawn!" the red putto laughed.

"He'll have to be ... to keep from screwing this up," the white putto said.

"But can he be?" the red putto deadpanned.

They laughed. Each putto dipped a hand into the holy water fountain and crossed himself. Still laughing and looking at each other, not where they were flying, they slammed into the door as Julius closed it on them. They hit the floor.

Outside of Switzerland's Chateau de Ranged, lightning flashed in an early morning wind-driven rainstorm. Inside, the Council of the Reserve Guard, ex-Vatican guards of varying ages and physical condition, awaited the pope. About two dozen men sat around, some clothed in various pieces of Vatican guard or military uniforms; some were in street clothes. Many drank from bottles and flasks.

They cheered two men who arm wrestled. Both were big and rugged; one was much younger than the other. They fought evenly until one man's arm began to waver. Finally, the back of the man's hand smacked the table. Cheers went up, drinks went down. Good-natured slaps on the back followed and money changed hands. Helmut, the older man, ruffled Damian's shaggy hair.

"Damian, you were always the best, and the strongest still," Helmet complimented.

"Nein, Helmut. I was never a match for you in your prime and hardly one now," Damian said deferentially.

"Then why didn't you let me win?" Helmut asked, as all the guards laughed.

A big door slammed. Boots crunched the stone floor. Men quickly drained their drinks and stashed their cash. Some straightened their clothes. One leaned drunkenly against a wall.

Two silhouettes appeared in an arched hallway. Julius and Sarge came into the light and walked toward the guards. The guards bowed their heads. Julius walked to one of the men, who knelt to kiss his ring.

"Kiss ass," Helmut whispered to Damian with a smile.

"Get up, Lex," Julius said.

The pope grabbed Lex by the shoulders, pulled him up and gave him a hug. Everyone gathered around for a raucous greeting. Julius, Sarge and the ex-guards slapped shoulders and shook hands as they exchanged greetings. Julius had met most of them at their annual reunion the year before.

"Let's have a drink," Julius said, getting a flask from his coat.

Julius continued. "A toast. Gentlemen, I am in your service. Many of you, as young Vatican guards, served my Father when he was pope. I salute you."

The men cheered and drank. Julius sat down at a thick table with some of the men.

"Your loyalty and allegiance are beyond any blessing. Now I ask you to go on one more mission, one last quest of Biblical proportions – to recover the crown jewels of the papacy, the Tiara of Julius II. History, legacy hang in the balance."

"I'm getting a woody," Otto, an old veteran, pronounced.

Julius continued. "There's only one problem. I have no idea where it is. You are the most loyal soldiers in the world. Sarge and I want three of you to travel with us and find it. Any volunteers?"

"We'll follow you to the ends of the earth, Your Holiness," Helmut contended.

Most of the other guards shouted in agreement.

Julius smiled. "Great, because that's where we're going...to Gypsylvania."

The guards went silent and still, then into complete disarray. Those able-bodied enough flew from their chairs, bashing into each other as they tried to get out of the room. With hands on his hips, Julius blocked their escape. A cacophony of excuses echoed in the room as the men cowered before him.

"Can't milord."

"So sorry."

"I have a doctor's appointment."

"My wife is deathly ill."

"My son is leaving for the service."

"Family funeral, sir."

"Daughter is getting married, Your Holiness."

"My back just went out."

"C'mon now, men," Sarge admonished. "Belly up."

Julius addressed the soldiers. "Men, friends, I look around this room and I am humbled. Your lives, your careers, your blood represent the finest of Christendom. Linus, how often did you taste my father's food to assure its safety for him?"

Linus licked the fat fingers of one hand while holding a piece of chicken in the other. "More than I can count, milord," he shrugged.

"And you, Cornelius, you never shirked from the sting of battle," Julius said.

"Not once, milord," the blind Cornelius agreed.

Julius spoke to Matthew, a very old man asleep in a wheel chair who wore a Viking helmet.

"Matthew, no one has served God and pope longer or more nobly than you," Julius affirmed.

Helmut shook him awake.

"No one longer, Your Holiness," Matthew muttered. Then he tipped back into his chair, pulled a blanket over his shoulders and went back to sleep.

Julius jumped atop a stage in front of a giant papal flag. He held black leather gloves in one hand and smacked the other with them periodically as he addressed the men. The men looked up at him.

"There is only one thing standing in the way of getting back Julius II's Tiara," Julius explained, "a) knowing who the mastermind is and b) knowing where the tiara is. This journey, this quest, is neither crusade nor charade. We aren't promoting or pretending anything. Hell, it's not even about religion ~ at least I don't think it is. What it is about is as pure and simple as, well, as pure and simple as this beer here."

He pointed to a bottle on a table.

The guards boisterously respond, "Here! Here!"

Julius continued. "Someone stole Julius II's Tiara and by God, by the Son of God and by the Mother of God, I am going to get it back."

The men cast their eyes down, looking dejected, ashamed.

"If I have to get it back alone I will. And I will get it back. But I am willing to take Sarge and three of you with me to share in this god-given adventure to the most god-forsaken places on Earth. And return to glory the everlasting glory of God. Who's with me?" Julius asked.

No man budged.

"You are the best soldiers in the world," Julius affirmed.

Still nothing.

The putti hovered around Julius' head, dressed as little generals.

"They're pussies," the red putto proclaimed.

"Was 1527 a fluke?" Julius asked, referring to the Sack of Rome.

"That was before their time," the white putto explained.

Still nothing.

Julius paused. "Alright then. I excommunicate every one of you," he said and turned his back on them.

"I knew you had the excommunication card!" the white putto said ecstatically.

"Well played," said the red putto.

Every guard began to recant simultaneously.

"I'm in, Your Holiness."

"I'll go."

"I'm good for it."

"We aren't there yet?"

"Why didn't you say so?"

"Time to go to work."

"I'm ready."

"Let's do this."

Julius walked amid the men. He grabbed shoulders, necks and shook hands, then he sat down at the large table again.

"I knew you were all with me," he said, choking up a bit. "Sarge, take charge."

"Alright, men, circle up," Sarge ordered. " You can't all go. You have to draw straws. The three short straws go."

The draw began. Men broke out in a sweat. One man sighed in relief when he got a long straw. Damian, the young and strong guard, drew a short straw. He chuckled wryly.

"Ha! Good thing I don't want to live forever. Take care of my family for me, Helmut." Damian said.

"You won't live forever with that straw," Helmut said sympathetically. "Go with God."

Matthew, the old man in the Viking helmet, drew a long straw. Others patted him on the back.

Skinny, seventy-year-old Otto got up as Sarge walked to him with the handful of straws. Otto's skinny arms protruded from his dingy T-shirt and overalls. His almost toothless mouth and head twisted. He closed one eye and squinted out of the other as he drew. It was a shortie.

"Yahoo!" Otto hollered gleefully.

"Otto, the short straws go," Helmut explained.

Others nodded to Otto as the old man glanced about furtively. He passed out and hit the floor with a loud thump.

"Jesus," Sarge said.

Two more long straws were drawn. Then Adrian, a thirty-five year old impeccably dressed in a three-piece suit and considered by the others to be the smartest, picked his. It was a shortie.

"The odds were against me," Adrian reasoned.

"So were the gods," Lex added.

"That's it, the three straws. The rest of you are in reserve," Sarge said.

Adrian got smelling salts from his vest. He knelt by Otto and put them under Otto's nose. Otto's head snapped up. Sarge and Damian stood above them.

With hands on hips, Julius happily appraised the four men who were going with him.

"We shall be known as The Fellowship of the Tiara!" he said proudly.

A cheer went up from all who were not chosen.

Chapter X

Gypsylvania

THE PAPAL LEAR jet landed at an abandoned military airbase. Nearby mountains were silhouetted by a dim moon. The Lear taxied to an old hangar.

Alfonso, a heavily bearded eastern Orthodox priest, awaited them in the hangar. He was dressed in black and barely visible in the dark. A string of five horses and two packs mules were picketed nearby. Julius led Eli out of the plane. Sarge, Damian, Adrian and Otto walked behind them, carrying gear. "Alfonso," Julius said affectionately to the priest. Alfonso spoke with a heavy Balkan accent. "Julius – welcome. Good to see you again. Welcome gentlemen."

They exchanged handshakes and greetings.

"Do you need food? Rest?" Alfonso asked.

"No. We are ready to travel," Julius replied.

Alfonso looked around. "The Russians claim these mountains," he said. "We must be careful. The witches are a hard four-day ride away. Trust nothing in these woods," Alonzo continued. "Nothing is as it seems."

"Let's go," Julius said with a smile.

Within half an hour, the gear was loaded and the men saddled up. Moonlight barely revealed a sign that said: "Welcome to Gypsylvania – the end of the road starts here."

The trail soon narrowed and went up a steep mountain pass. It began to drizzle, then rain, then storm. The footing was treacherous; even the mules stumbled. The men rode through the night and into a very dark, ancient forest as they descended the first pass. The trail turned to mud as the rain continued, chilling the party to the bone. The men often passed human remains, skeletons mostly, and abandoned gear.

Ghoulish shadows followed them during the day, which was barely lighter than the nights. Specters, monstrous bats and vampire-like creatures harassed them at night. They swooped about their heads, and darted into camp, tipping soup and coffee pots and made it almost impossible to keep a fire going. The men were on edge, except for Julius. They slept little, having to keep watch on the horses and camp.

Julius arrowed several of the filthiest creatures and those kind stopped coming around. On the third night, however, something new took their place, as a loud noise slapped the wet forest floor beyond the light of the smoky campfire. Otto, who was hanging clothes to dry by the fire, quickly turned around. Everyone looked in the same direction of darkness.

"What was that?" he asked nervously.

"Check it out," Alfonso said.

"No way. It was probably a troll or something," Otto said.

"It wasn't a troll," said Adrian.

"How do you know?" asked Damian.

"Trolls are in Scandinavia, not this neck of the woods, so to speak," Adrian explained. "Besides, they are afraid of lightning. Thor used it to kill them, so there aren't many left. They'd never be out in weather like this."

"Then it's a Willymonger," Otto insisted.

"I'm afraid not. The Willymonger is limited to a very small range of moor in the British Isles," Adrian said.

"Then you tell me," Otto said defiantly.

"I'd say something more akin to a shape-shifting hala, with as hard as it's raining. Hali have stalked us all day, so I imagine it's one, or more, of them," Adrian explained.

"I'll go if you go," Otto said to Damian.

Damian replied, "I may be strong, but I'm not stupid."

"C'mon," Otto pleaded.

Damian exhaled loudly, got up and followed Otto into the shadows.

"Remember," Alonzo reminded. "Nothing is as it seems."

Julius, Sarge, Adrian and Alonzo stared into the fire.

Soon Alonzo spoke. "We've already made it farther than most who come this way. Nothing those two find out there will rival the witches. What possesses you to see those old women, Julius?"

"Those 'old women' belong to a lineage of ancient wisdom on which the Vatican was founded," Julius replied. "Not only was Vatican Hill the site of Nero's Circus, it was also where fortune tellers prophesied and healers sold charms to the Romans. As a matter of fact, the word Vatican is just a shortened form of the word *Vaticanus*. It is taken from two Latin words: *vates*, which means "tellers of fortune," and *anus*, which means "old woman." Basically, Vatican means 'hill of prophecy' and why an old woman initially represented the Church."

"Sounds like *Vaticanus* means an old woman talking out of her ass," Adrian mused.

"A perfect interpretation," Alfonso said.

Julius laughed a bit and continued. "You hear things when you become pope," Julius explained. "Julius II was the fortune tellers' greatest benefactor, but they fell out of favor with later popes. These two witches, as you call them, were kicked out in the 14th century with the others. They are the last ones alive. They left peacefully, but formed a symbiotic relationship with the papacy. Every pope is obliged to see them at least once and the witches are obliged to help ... for a price."

"So, what do you need from them?" asked Alfonso.

"Magic," Julius said with a smile. "Magic is what gives the hero's snowball a chance in hell."

Just then, Damian came running back to the fire screaming, with Otto lagging behind. A demonic host of flying and running shadows and creatures pursued them. Julius quickly nocked an arrow. Alfonso drew a sword. Sarge and Adrian drew pistols. Otto's raincoat flapped open as he ran past the fire, looking over his shoulder. He tripped over the firewood, twisted and fell on his back. His coat flew open, exposing his white, wrinkled body. The firelight revealed that all he wore was a red thong.

The demons stopped in mid flight and stride. Then, as quickly as they came, they vaporized into the night. Otto got up tentatively, then proudly held his coat open wide.

Nodding his head he said, "That's right. You need to be man or woman enough to handle this." He turned 360 degrees, grinning.

"Otto! Cover it up!" Sarge barked as he threw Otto's pants at him.

"I won't be able to sleep tonight after seeing that," Alfonso chuckled.

"Nobody could sleep before we saw that," reasoned Julius.

After almost two more days of stormy travel, the Fellowship approached a small cabin built into a mountain. The light was fading. The men could barely make out a weathered sign over the cabin that read 'Will Divine for Gold.'

"Therein lie the most mad and maddening women in the world," Alfonso said to the party. Then he turned to Julius. "You still want to go through with this?"

Damian got off his horse and marched toward the cabin's porch.

"After all this shit? Of course we're going through with this," he said vehemently. He ran up the porch steps, then knocked hard on the door.

"No! No!" Alfonso yelled as he jumped off his horse.

"Let him go," Julius said.

Alfonso stopped. Damian pounded on the door. There was no reply.

"Keep knocking, Damian. I don't think they hear you yet," Sarge said satirically.

Finally, the door slowly squeaked opened. An unkempt, gray-haired, short, powerfully built old woman came into view. She wore a brown shawl, tattered gray skirt, fingerless black gloves and black boots. She levitated to Damian's height, looked at him innocently, smiled sweetly, then smacked him in the side of the head. He tumbled off the porch and into the wet grass.

The witch settled down on the porch. "What are you trying to do?" she hissed through clenched, yellow teeth. "Piss off the Russians?"

"No. Sorry," Damian stammered. "I'm ..." he said slowly as he pointed at Julius, "the pope ..."

Another old woman's voice came from inside the cabin. "Who is it, dear?"

The old woman on the porch looked inside and said, "Some dumbass who says he's the pope."

Another woman came to the doorway. She looked almost exactly like the first witch. She scrutinized Damian.

"He doesn't look like much," she said.

"They never do," the first witch replied.

"Let him in," said the second witch.

Damian got up and walked to the door.

"Not until he apologizes," the first witch said angrily.

"I'm sorry," Damian said quickly.

"Ha! For what?" the first witch challenged.

"For knocking so hard," Damian said apologetically.

"And?"

"And for pissing off the Russians?" Damian asked

"And?" the first witch pushed.

"For god sakes, woman, I don't know. For whatever you want," Damian said defiantly.

"Not good enough" the first witch pronounced. She scurried inside and slammed the door in his face.

Inside, the witches walked from the door, arm in arm. "Who was at the door, dear?" asked the second witch.

"Some dumbass who says he's the pope," replied the first.

Outside, Damian looked at the others, then got ready to knock again.

"Let me try," Julius said.

Julius slipped off Eli and walked to the door. He pulled out a leather pouch from inside his coat and shook it lightly.

The women inside looked at each other excitedly.

Julius jingled the pouch every so slightly again.

The witches ran back to the door and opened it.

"Yes?" asked the first witch sweetly.

"I'm sorry, madam. We bothered you by mistake," Julius said as he held the pouch to her face.

The witch grabbed for it, but Julius snatched it away from her.

"We shall take our leave," Julius said as he turned.

Quickly, the witch appeared in front of Julius as he prepared to walk down the porch steps.

"No, come in," she said. "Who are we to let weary travelers leave without offering food and shelter?"

"We don't have time," Julius said. "We are looking for two women who might help us with a divination request. Evidently we made a mistake coming here. I apologize."

"This request, will you pay for it?" the first witch asked demurely.

"In gold," Julius replied.

The second witch came to the doorway. "Please forgive my sister, kind sir," she said. "We are the ones for whom you are looking. I am Bella. This is my sister, Stella. We two helpless women live alone. With the Russians nearby, we can't be too careful."

"I'm familiar with the Russians," Julius empathized.

"And the Cossacks," Bella spat. "May the pox be on them. We thought you might be Cossacks, but none ever had a horse as fine as yours. Please, come in." She motioned Julius and the others inside.

Julius turned to the men. "Damian, Adrian, stay with the horses," he said.

On the outside, the witches' cabin looked very small. Inside, it was huge. The men ogled it as they walked down a dim and dusty, cobweb-covered hall. The witches led Julius, Sarge, Otto and Alfonso to a candle lit room filled with shelves of jars, cases of books, and a menagerie of stuffed and live animals – a wolf, cats, owls, a vulture, monkeys, frogs, leeches – and plants. A large cauldron steamed in the middle of the room. Droppings, fur and feathers littered the floor.

"Have a seat," Bella said, motioning to chairs in a semicircle around the cauldron.

A combination of dank and sulfuric smells permeated the air. A crackling fire in a wood stove somewhat heated the room.

Stella rubbed her hands delightedly. "Shall we talk business first?"

"You need to be aware of our no-guarantee policy," Bella said.

"And anything we say can and will be used against you," Stella added.

"Plus, we need gold up front," added Bella.

"Not upfront," Julius countered. "Do your work and you will be rewarded. As a token of trust, however, I will give each of you a gold coin."

Julius held up a large gold coin in each hand and leaned forward. The witches snatched them quickly.

Stella appraised the coin. "A gold coin ... from The Vatican?"

Bella bit hers and tried to bend it. She took it out of her mouth and said, "So, you're pope now?"

"I am," Julius confirmed.

"You look a lot like a pope who was here," Stella turned to Bella and asked, "What ... maybe thirty, thirty-five years ago?"

"That would have been my father," Julius said.

The witches laughed.

Bella nudged Stella and confided, "The Vatican may be crazier now than when we lived there."

Stella leaned toward Julius. "Oh, your father was a keeper. He said he was from the Dioceses of Mephistopheles. Paid us well in more ways than one, if you know what I mean and I know you do. He came to us to find you. And now look who's here, look who's pope. You...you glorious bastard!"

"We do good work," Bella added.

"So did he!" Stella laughed.

"I'm sure he did," Julius said. "Now, let's go."

Stella straightened her skirt. "Once we start, everyone must stay seated," she said.

"And don't touch anything metal," Bella instructed.

"I need to find someone who took something," Julius said.

The witches looked at each other and laughed. "He sounds just like his father," they said in unison.

The witches stood up and began to speak in rhymes and alternate lines. They cavorted and weaved about the pope.

"Toads? Tarots?"

"Or do you want I read your palm?"

"Sorcery? Astrology?"

"One or both can bring you calm."

"Enchantments? Enhancements?"

"Protection for your encampments?"

"Or a carry-along charm to keep you from harm?"

"Tell me, what's your fancy?"

"Speak with the dead through necromancy?"

"Spells of wealth? Spells of leisure?"

"Something wicked with which to please her?"

Stella held up a French Tickler.

"Perhaps a potion? A lotion?"

"You'll love what we can put into motion."

Both witches seductively swayed their hips.

"A trance for romance starts with a li'l witch's lap dance," the witches said together.

Stella tried to sit on Julius' lap. He pushed her away.

Otto wiped drool from the corner of his mouth.

"I'd love to get into that witch's brew," he said.

The witches went back to alternating lines.

"Wizards?"

"Gizzards?"

"Tails of..."

"Lizards?"

"Or the truth from frog entrails?"

"Don't like their smell or annoyance?"

"You may prefer clairvoyance."

"Conjure or conjuration?"

"Pick your poison, Holy One."

"All we need is a small donation."

The witches concluded together and innocently, "Or do you want it all?"

"She left this," Julius said and handed the parkour flag shot from La-Trelle's shorts.

The witches studied it for a few moments as they mumbled to each other, then Bella dropped the flag into the cauldron. Stella grabbed Julius's hand and held it over the cauldron. She pulled a knife from her belt and sliced Julius' hand with it, spilling his blood into the pot. A phantom-like scene appeared in the steam above it.

"Nappy!" Julius exclaimed virulently.

The men watched spellbound as Nappy admired the tiara, perched on a hat stand. A veritable twin of Napoleon Bonaparte, Nappy had short, dark hair on a round head and small eyes. Dressed like the historic Napoleon, Nappy wore a green Chasseurs à Cheval coat, beige shirt, white pants and black knee-high boots. He primped in front of a mirror, adjusted his collar, then reached for the tiara.

Julius pushed himself slightly up in the chair. "Don't touch the tiara, Nappy," he growled.

"Sit down!" Bella warned.

Julius was oblivious to her. "Don't try to put it on," he said.

Nappy put the tiara above his head, only to absorb a huge shock to his hands and head. Sparks danced around him. He could not get the tiara close to his head.

"Yeow!" he hollered. "The prophecy. *Sacre bleu!*" he said with a heavy French accent.

Julius remained focused on Nappy. "Put it down," he said emphatically, as he stood up completely.

"No!" the witches hollered together and reached toward Julius.

Julius leaned toward Alfonso, drew the man's sword and jumped onto the cauldron. He slashed through the apparition and knocked over the cauldron.

Far away in his quarters, Nappy saw a sword come at him out of thin air, with no one holding it. He fell backwards, with arms up protectively.

"Aaaaaaaaaaaaargh!" he shrieked

The witches reached for Julius. Thunder and lightning and screaming filled the air. Winds tore through the room, scattering the witches' belongings. There was tremendous flash, and then everything went black.

Julius lay in bed with an ice bag on his head. A snake slithered over him. An owl hooted on a bedpost. Hummingbirds fluttered about the room. The witches and men stood over him. Finally, Julius slowly opened his eyes.

"Dumbass Pope," Bella chided.

"Pope Dumbass," pronounced Stella.

"Too stupid to pray ..." Bella said.

"... so he came to us," concluded Stella.

"Stay in the chair,' we told him," Bella continued.

"'Don't touch anything metal,' we said," reminded Stella.

"So what does he do?" asked Bella.

"Jumps up with a sword," Stella answered.

"Stupid Pope," Stella confirmed.

"Pope Stupid," Bella christened.

"We're all lucky to be alive," Stella admonished.

"Especially you," agreed Bella.

"Stupid you," Stella said.

"As strong as he is stupid," Bella continued.

"As stupid as he is strong," Stella mocked.

"Lucky fuck, he is," Bella added

"Fucking lucky," Stella agreed.

"We need more gold to pay for this," Bella appraised.

"At least twice as much," Stella affirmed.

Julius painfully got out of bed. He handed Stella a purse from his vest pocket.

"It's yours," he said.

The witches looked inside the purse and were ecstatic. They looked at each other and said, "Like his father, he is!"

Julius, trying to gather his strength, turned to Sarge and said, "I know where the tiara is. Let's go."

The Fellowship of the Tiara rode away from the witches' cabin. For the first time on the trip, the sun shined.

"What happened?" Sarge asked.

"When I jumped on the cauldron, I was in two places at once. Alfonso's sword pulled me forward; something else kept me back. But I clearly saw Nappy. He has the tiara in the old papal palace in Avignon, *Le Palais des Papes*," Julius said.

"*Le Palais des Papes*?" Sarge repeated.

"*Oui*, the Palace of the Popes," Julius explained.

"And Nappy is?" Sarge asked.

"The great-great-great-great-great grandson of Napoleon Bonaparte," Julius replied.

"Nappy," Otto drawled derisively. "I should have killed him. Your father stopped me."

"I haven't thought of Nappy in years. He and I were in the seminary together. On a trip to Paris he tried to steal the Tiara of Julius II when it was at the Louvre. Security caught him. Nappy was kicked out of the seminary. He blamed me because I did not put a good word in for him to my father. I heard he became an art dealer."

Julius put Eli into a canter. "To Avignon!" he cried.

"Let's get out of Gypsylvania first," Alfonso said quietly.

Chapter XI

Bless me, Father

IN THE EARLY evening four days later, the Fellowship waited near a bridge on the opposite bank of the Rhone River from *Le Palais des Papes*. Lying on their stomachs in the grass behind a small knoll, Julius and Sarge spied on the castle through binoculars. Julius wore sunglasses, a sahariane and his shirt collar up to partially hide his face.

The putti flew around in disguises comparable to Julius'. The guards wore their standard blue uniforms. Damian sat cross-legged behind Julius and Sarge, studying a sheet of paper. Otto practiced tai chi nearby.

"Care to know the results from the Julius Games, Your Holiness?" Damian asked.

"Yes, please. Who took the overall?" Julius asked.

"The Benedictines of Santo Domingo," Damian answered.

"That's great! Who won the horseback archery?" Julius queried.

"Let's see. Goktanri, the Hun," Damian replied.

"He's good," Julius conceded. "How did Niklas do in the strength events?"

Damian checked the paper. "Third. Lutherans took the first two spots."

"Not bad," Julius said.

Julius and Sarge continued to watch the castle through binoculars.

"We need to find a way in, in case Adrian does not make it back soon," Julius finally said.

"Your Holiness. Look. A priest," Otto said.

An old priest rode a burro toward the bridge. He wore a black cassock, cape and wide brim black hat. Julius and Sarge lowered their binoculars.

"My God. Just what we need," Julius affirmed.

Julius got up. He, Eli and the others jogged toward the priest as he neared the bridge.

"Father!" Julius hailed.

Startled at seeing men suddenly run toward him, the priest nevertheless stopped his burro.

"Yes, my good man?" the priest asked a bit guardedly.

"Are you going into the palace?" Julius asked excitedly.

"Yes," the priest replied. "I've been asked to hear confession there."

"Really? I, too, am a priest," Julius confided. "The owner of the palace is an old friend. I'd like to surprise him. May I trade places with you?"

"You? A priest?" the priest asked. "Doesn't seem possible."

The priest put his heels into the burro's ribs and tried to ride past Julius and the others. Sarge grabbed the burro's halter and stopped it.

"Your Holiness, your ring," Sarge said to Julius.

"Oh, yeah," Julius said, then he turned to the priest. "One moment, Father. I was just in Gypsylvania. One doesn't wear something like this in Gypsylvania. This may help convince you."

Julius took off his sunglasses, put his shirt collar down, removed the papal ring from the gold chain around his neck and put it on his finger. The priest was astonished.

"Most Holy Father," he said deferentially. "I am deeply sorry. I did not recognize you. I am Father Michael."

The priest got off his burro. Both he and the burro prostrated themselves before the pope. Julius helped him up.

"No problem, *mon père*," Julius comforted. "Just let me borrow your cassock so I can hear my friend's confession."

"With all due respect, Your Holiness, I can't," the priest said. "I was the one called. You, yourself, say we must all respond when our sheep bleah for help."

"As the Vicar of Christ, I exonerate you from this responsibility," Julius replied kindly.

"But Your Holiness ..." the priest protested.

"Oh, for Christ's sakes, Father, you leave me no choice," Julius said impatiently. "Seize him."

"Your Holiness!" the priest exclaimed.

Sarge and Damian grabbed, gagged and stripped the priest to his underwear, then tied him beneath the bridge in the shade. Otto got on all fours, snarled in the priest's face and threateningly sliced a finger across his own throat.

Julius took Otto by the collar and gently pulled him away. Then Julius crouched next to the priest.

"Sorry, Father. I'll let you hear my confession later to make this up to you. I'll have a lot to say when this is over." Then to the others Julius said, "I'm going in."

"We can't let you go in alone," Sarge protested.

"God is with me," Julius said.

"God is with us, too. You'll have more God with you with us with you," Sarge countered.

"True," Julius conceded. "What do you propose?"

The men were interrupted by a shiny white cleaning service van that pulled up to the bridge. Painted on the sides was: "HEAVEN SENT CLEANING – God Helps Those Who Clean Themselves." Adrian got out of it.

"Your super modified popemobile, Your Holiness," Adrian said proudly.

"Nice work, Adrian," Julius complimented.

"It looks like a cleaning van, but it's so much more," Adrian explained. "Look. If the palace gate won't open for us, we can press this button."

Adrian pressed a button on a remote and a battering ram came out the front of the van. It looked like an angel. Angelic trumpet music played. He pressed it again and the ram disappeared.

"There's a bunch of other buttons on the dashboard," Adrian elaborated. "It'll be fun."

Julius stuck his head through a window and admired the popemobile interior. "This changes everything," he concluded.

"Now what's our plan, Holiness?" Sarge asked.

Julius turned around to answer Sarge. "Nappy's expecting a Father Confessor, so a Father Confessor he will get."

Julius strolled to Eli and with his knife, quickly cut some of Eli's tail. Eli shook his head, but complied.

Julius turned to Adrian and asked, "Adrian, can you find something in the van to attach a beard?"

Adrian opened a small compartment in the wall of the van. He rifled through some medical supplies, then said, "There's skin glue in the first aid kit."

The men gathered around Julius as Adrian fashioned and attached Eli's "facial hair" to him.

"Our plan, milord?" Sarge asked.

Julius spoke while Adrian tried to stick a goatee on his chin. "I'll hear Nappy's confession and get him to tell me where the tiara is. Sarge, you'll come with me. Adrian, you, Damian and Otto secure a way out of the palace, then meet Sarge and me in the chapel. Then we'll get the tiara. Be discreet."

Soon Julius sported bushy eyebrows, mutton chop sideburns and a goatee. He pulled his sahariane on and wrapped up in the priest's cape.

Adrian handed Julius a mirror. Julius turned his face from side to side as he checked his reflection.

Satisfied, he said, "This is going to be easy."

With his disguise and plan in place, Julius rode Eli to the front gate guard station of *Le Palais des Papes*. Sarge rode along side of him on the priest's mule. They stopped at the guard station's barricade. All of Nappy's troops wore Napoleonic-era uniforms. Nappy's logo was on the front of each of their shirts, a hand partially tucked inside of a shirt.

A security guard stepped out of the guard station and asked, "Your business?"

Julius humbly removed his hat and replied, "The master of the castle has asked that I, Father Michael, hear his confession."

The guarded nodded at Sarge. "And that takes two of you?"

"Brother Martin is here to preach to the choir," Julius said deferentially.

The guard checked a list on his clipboard, then pointed his thumb in the direction of the Palace as the barricade raised. "Enter," he said.

The main castle gate swung open. Julius and Sarge rode into a courtyard and were met by another guard. The gate closed behind them.

"Follow me, please," the courtyard guard said. "I'll take you to the chapel. Leave your mounts here."

As Julius, Sarge and the guard walked off, the cleaning van pulled up to the guard station in front of the palace. Adrian, Otto and Damian, dressed like janitors, were inside.

The guard looked into the van and asked again, "Your business?"

Adrian was at the wheel. He answered, "To clean the chateau."

"One moment," the guard said. He glanced at his clipboard. "You aren't scheduled until tomorrow," he pronounced.

"We had a cancellation in the neighborhood, so came by today," Adrian said confidently. "The owner will receive a 10% discount if we can work here now."

Then guard went inside the guard station and got on the phone. When he returned, the castle gate swung open again.

The guard stuck his head out the doorway. "Enter," he said.

Adrian drove the van inside.

"Sonovabitch!" Otto scowled. " I was ready to off that prick."

"Settle down," Damian counseled. "Be discreet."

Inside the palace chapel, the guard opened the confessional door for Julius. Julius smiled and blessed the man with a sign of the cross.

"Thank you, my son," he said.

Julius entered the confessional, removed his sunglasses, kissed the stole and put it over his head. He kept the door slightly open to keep an eye on Sarge, who knelt nearby at a side altar.

Julius appraised his confines. "Lord, help me. This confessional feels like an outhouse. With the tiara so close I'm ready to crap my pants."

Julius soon heard voices. He peeked outside the confessional door and saw Nappy walk into the chapel with Sister LaTrelle. Nappy wore a Napoleonic uniform; LaTrelle wore traditional nun's clothing and white cornette.

Julius studied the pair, then quietly said to himself, "It is the same La-Trelle. She always did look good in a little black dress."

Julius sat up straight just before Nappy entered the confessional. He watched through the confessional screen as Nappy crossed himself.

"Hello, my son," Julius said softly.

"*Bonjour*," Nappy replied. "Bless me, Father, for I have sinned. My last confession was over twenty years ago."

"Whoa," Julius commented. "Sounds as if we may be here for a while. Let me get more comfortable."

Julius adjusted himself, then said, "Continue."

"Father," Nappy began, "I took something that doesn't belong to me."

"The Universe is forgiving not for getting," Julius counseled. "So give it back and ask God for forgiveness. What did you take?"

"It's difficult to say, Father," Nappy replied.

"It is important to confess the grievousness of the taking," Julius urged.

"I began to steal long ago," Nappy said. "The guilt haunts me."

"There is no transformational value in guilt, my son," Julius said.

Nappy continued. "It began quite innocently, quite small, with the taking of ceremonial wine from the sacristy when I was an altar boy."

Julius chuckled. "I did the same. Priests at the monastery near where I lived made a very good chardonnay. Come to think of it, I've never confessed that. Still, I prefer a nice pinot."

Nappy gained momentum as he spoke. "Stealing became my way of dealing with my family's stolen place in history, by history. My family has a long and regal story, although some would say short and ignominious simply because it is associated with one teeny, weenie-weenie little loss, Waterloo."

As Julius looked around the confessional absently listening to Nappy, he happened to peek through the slightly open confessional door and saw LaTrelle studying Sarge at the side altar.

"Uh-oh," Julius said.

"Oui," Nappy agreed.

At the side altar, LaTrelle eyed Sarge suspiciously. She walked around, studying him. Sarge looked straight ahead.

"You look familiar, but out of place," LaTrelle said finally.

Sarge continued to look straight ahead, but answered, "I feel the same about you."

"What's your business?" LaTrelle demanded.

"To preach to the choir. Now shhhh!" Sarge hissed.

"Don't shhhh me," LaTrelle warned.

"SHHHHHH!" Sarge said more loudly When he turned away from her, LaTrelle grabbed his shoulder.

"Don't give me that," she told him.

Inside the confessional, Nappy still recalled history. "My great-great-great-great-great grandfather came within a whisker, within a gnat's ass, within a pimple on a gnat's ass, within a whisker in a pimple on a gnat's ass of bringing Europe and the Catholic Church to their knees."

Julius listened to Nappy, but watched LaTrelle and Sarge.

"But how does one steal back one's rightful place in history?" Nappy asked sincerely.

Julius faced the confessional screen and became more attentive. "That's not the kind of question I should answer in the confessional," he said. "You don't have to steal. Just rewrite history. Make stuff up. The Church does it often enough." "

Ha," Nappy sneered. "I'm about to steal victory from those who stole it from my great-great-great -great-great grandfather."

"Why don't you just say Napoleon?" Julius questioned.

"People don't realize my great-great-great ... Napoleon, as Emperor of Europe, had the right to name the pope," Napoleon revealed.

"Not quite. The pope had the right to name the Emperor of the Holy Roman Empire, which was neither Holy, nor Roman nor an Empire," Julius quipped.

"Doesn't matter," Nappy responded. "What better place to steal back my family's place in history than in a confessional? As Napoleon's heir, I have the right to name the pope."

Julius sat back from the screen into his chair and said quietly to himself, "But no right to steal from the pope, you little prick."

Julius leaned forward to the screen again. "My son, I sense there is something else troubling you. Something else you have taken and wish to return."

"Nope. I don't think so," Nappy said after some thought. "Nothing."

Adrian, Damian and Otto were in the popemobile parked in a palace corridor. They went through its contents.

"Holy crap! Look at all this stuff. Guns. Vests. Ammo. Grenades," Damian said merrily.

"We are part of the most elite fighting force in the world," Adrian affirmed.

"Oooo-wee! I'm getting a woody!" Otto announced.

Adrian and Damian looked at each other dubiously.

"Look. Really. I am getting a woody." Otto proudly pointed both hands to the erection in his pants.

"You better quit pointing at it if you don't want it shot off," Damian said.

"Let's go to work," Adrian said.

The three men suited up with bulletproof vests that looked like the formal blue, red and orange striped Vatican Guard uniforms. VATICAN GUARD lettering was on the back. They holstered pistols, strapped on ammo belts and grabbed MP5 submachine guns.

"Otto," Adrian said, "Damian and I will go forward to secure a corridor. Bring up the rear with extra ammo. Be discreet."

Adrian and Damian began a series of S.W.A.T.-like moves. They stealthily worked their way toward a small vestibule off the main corridor where four of Nappy's soldiers were posted. Otto struggled behind them, carrying extra gear and being ruddered by the woody projecting from his pants. Adrian and Damian crouched near the vestibule, hidden by a corner of a wall. When the four soldiers were in the right position, Adrian and Damian attacked them. Each man took on two soldiers, slamming their heads together. All four fell to the floor stunned. Adrian and Damian gagged and taped them, and secured them out of the way.

Unknown to them, Sister Susan noticed them on a screen in the Palace Monitoring Center when Otto stood over Nappy's soldiers and flexed his biceps.

"What the hell?" she asked herself. Then she spoke into a microphone. "There's a breach. Get security to Section 8."

Dozens of Napoleonic soldiers immediately ran down hallways toward the Vatican guards, grouping together like streams coming together to make a river.

Meanwhile, Julius continued hearing Nappy's confession.

"After twenty years away from the confessional, there must be something else," Julius said to Nappy, as he pushed his slipping goatee not quite back into place. "Search your heart," Julius urged. Then he leaned back from the confessional screen and mumbled to himself, "Better yet, let me search your quarters."

Nappy looked and felt dejected, embracing the guilt-provoking power of confessing his sins. "I've been out of control my whole life," he said, and his head and shoulders slumped.

"Can a man who's never been in control be out of control?" Julius asked lightly.

"Why, no!" Nappy affirmed merrily.

"Then forget about it," Julius said. "Moderation in all things, including excess, I always say."

"I like you, *mon père*," Nappy said. "If the penance you give me is not too onerous, perchance we can share a bottle of wine this evening. I have several fine pinots at the *palais*. I also make a mean equine pate'."

Julius scowled. "Horsemeat pate'?" he asked.

"*Mais Oui!*" Nappy answered happily. "It's quite the delicacy."

Julius erupted, no longer trying to disguise his voice. "That will send you to hell for all time, suffering in the grip of the Legions of Satan!"

"I know that voice," Nappy said alarmingly, as he squinted through the confessional screen to study the priest sitting across from him.

In Julius' heightened agitation, his goatee slipped again. He tried to stick it into place.

As he watched Julius, Nappy finally put the face and voice together. "*Mon Dieu. Julius!*" he cried.

On the other side of the chapel, LaTrelle and Sarge heard Julius and Nappy yelling. They saw the confessional rock back and forth. Then Nappy opened the confessional door and tried to run away. Julius hurled his torso through the confessional screen and grabbed Nappy by the throat before he could escape.

"Damn it, Nappy. Give me the tiara!" Julius bellowed.

Nappy's eyes popped out as Julius squeezed his throat tighter. Nappy looked to LaTrelle.

"Help!" he said hoarsely.

LaTrelle stripped off the white cornette from her head. She tugged on it and quickly fashioned it into a three feet long blowgun. Then she took a pin from her hair, put it in her mouth and blew a dart at Sarge.

Sarge slapped his neck.

"Bitch!" he spat and slumped unconscious to the floor.

LaTrelle ran toward the confessional.

Julius dropped a blue-faced Nappy and sized up LaTrelle. "Shit," he said. He wiggled out of the confessional screen, then he threw open his confessional door to confront her.

Nappy squirmed on the floor, gasping for breath. LaTrelle stopped within three meters of Julius. The tension was palpable. They spoke vilely to each other at the same time.

"LaTrelle ..."

"*Le Pape...*"

LaTrelle's hair fell as she removed another hairpin and blew it at Julius. Julius reacted quickly. He pulled Nappy up by his collar. Nappy took the dart in his jugular and went limp. Julius dropped him and rushed LaTrelle.

Another battle raged inside the serpentine palace corridor as soldiers rushed Adrian, Damian and Otto from several directions. Sisters Angela, Carmela and Marie, wearing traditional nun clothing, directed different columns of soldiers to attack positions.

"Back to the van!" Adrian ordered. "We'll ram them."

As both sides fired shots, Damian and Adrian retreated to the popemobile. Otto fell behind, struggling with gear. He stopped in a protected alcove. Adrian jumped behind the wheel and drove toward him. Bullets bounced off the armored popemobile and its windshield as Damian leaned out of the door and scooped up the old man as the soldiers closed in.

"Eat shit, you sons o' bitches!" Otto barked.

Damian turned to Adrian. "Where are we going?" he hollered.

Adrian pointed to a sign on the wall. It read *La Chapelle de Saint Michelle.* "The chapel to get His Holiness."

Sister Susan continued to watch the battle from the Palace Monitoring Center. As the popemobile rounded a bend, she pushed a button and dropped a steel gate across the corridor. She saw the popemobile's battering ram deploy and heard heavenly trumpets sound as the popemobile blasted through the gate. Nappy's soldiers flew out of its way as it hurled by.

"That pisses me off," Sister Susan hissed to herself.

Julius and LaTrelle squared off as they circled each other. Sarge was crumpled before the side altar. Nappy lay unconscious with his back against the confessional.

"Say your prayers, *pape*," LaTrelle told the pontiff.

"Bring it on, sista. I'm in a state of grace."

LaTrelle snapped kicks and punches. Julius defensively backpedaled, blocking everything she threw. When he tried to get her in an armlock, LaTrelle dropped under his elbow to her knees at his crotch.

"Ha! More like a state of excitement," she laughed derisively.

"Same thing," Julius corrected, as he grabbed her by the waist and lifted her over his head.

Her skirt fell over both their heads. Their eyes met again as Julius looked up and LaTrelle looked down.

"Uh-oh," they said simultaneously.

LaTrelle eye poked Julius. "Ow!" he growled as he dropped her.

LaTrelle slipped down Julius' chest and bent him forward with her knees around his ears. They rolled like a tire and crashed into the confessional. LaTrelle got the wind knocked out of her as she landed next to Nappy. Julius sprang up.

"Confess, LaTrelle. Where's the tiara?" he demanded.

LaTrelle looked up at Julius. "You owe me a pair of shorts."

"You owe me a tiara. Where is it?" Julius demanded again.

LaTrelle lifted her skirt and seductively spread her legs. "Look familiar?" she asked.

Julius looked at her long, smooth legs and the knife strapped to her thigh near a heart-shaped tattoo.

"The knife?" he asked innocently.

"You bastard!" she snarled.

"Even my mother calls me that," Julius said with mock sadness.

LaTrelle snatched the blowgun, and with lightning speed took the last pin from her hair and put it in her mouth.

Julius reached for her. LaTrelle blew the dart. Julius grabbed his neck, stumbled and fell face down in her lap. LaTrelle looked down triumphantly. She wrapped her fingers in his hair and tugged it.

"All too easy," she said triumphantly. "Perhaps you are not as strong as the Emperor thought."

The popemobile busted through the chapel door, then squealed to a stop. The guards surveyed the chapel. Damian pointed toward the confessional.

"His Holiness is down!" Damian hollered.

Adrian stepped on the gas. Tires squealed and spun as the van roared down the main aisle.

LaTrelle pushed Julius off and ran, but fell hard face down.

Julius had her ankle. He quickly straddled her back and pinned her arms behind her. He dropped the dart at her nose. He had caught it before it hit him.

"You missed, LaTrelle. Now, where is the tiara?" he asked again.

LaTrelle looked over her shoulder. "Is that all you care about?"

Julius lifted LaTrelle to her feet as he said, "I may be a bit preoccupied."

He turned her around. The two studied each other intensely.

"Why are you working for Nappy?" he asked gently.

"Because you forgot about me," LaTrelle answered angrily.

"I never forgot you ... or your eyes," Julius explained.

They relaxed and smiled at each other slightly. "But my thighs? You didn't recognize my thighs?" she asked coyly.

The popemobile spun in a circle at the intersection of two aisles, burning tires and crashing pews. Hung up on debris, and with tires smoking, it slowly headed toward the confessional.

Julius gently worked off one of his bushy eyebrows. "Your eyes haven't changed as much."

The gentleness in LaTrelle's voice masked the fire in her eyes. She tenderly put her hands on his face.

"Let me help," she offered.

She quickly ripped off the muttonchops. Julius blinked his slightly watering eyes. LaTrelle smiled.

"You're twisted, Sister."

LaTrelle scowled. She slapped Julius. His face snapped to the side.

"No one calls me a twisted sister, not even *le Pape*," LaTrelle said hotly.

Julius slowly recovered, then quickly slapped LaTrelle.

The red putto, dressed like LaTrelle, slapped the white putto, dressed like Julius.

LaTrelle slapped Julius.

The white putto slapped the red putto.

Julius slapped LaTrelle.

LaTrelle slapped at Julius. Julius caught her hand.

"You slap like a bishop," he chided.

Deftly, Julius spun and pinned LaTrelle to the confessional with his body, removed her waist sash and tied her arms behind her. She looked over her shoulder at Julius.

"Don't tie me up," she warned.

"You never complained before," Julius said as he laughed.

"We were on the same side then," LaTrelle snapped.

The popemobile roared up and stopped.

Julius looked at Damian. "Take her," he said and gently pushed La-Trelle toward him.

Damian pulled LaTrelle inside the van. Julius grabbed the unconscious Nappy and threw him onto a back seat.

Suddenly, Nappy's soldiers rushed in from the back and front of the chapel, and rappelled from the balcony.

Julius saw them coming. He turned to Otto and Damian, and pointed to Nappy and LaTrelle. "Tape their hands and feet, and into those seats," he said. To Adrian he added, "Let's get Sarge."

"Don't tape me down," LaTrelle said to Damian.

"I have to," Damian replied. "He's infallible."

Julius grabbed his bow and quiver hanging in the van. The van spun around the aisle and raced to the unconscious Sarge.

Sister Carmela and two soldiers pulled Sarge to his feet. Just as a soldier was about to put a pistol to Sarge's head, Julius drew an arrow. Bracing himself in the panel doorway on the right side of the van, Julius shot. The arrow knocked the pistol out of the soldier's hand.

Damian leaned out of the van, grabbed Sarge from the other soldier and hauled him in. The popemobile pealed away toward the front of the chapel. Adrian handed Damian smelling salts. Damian wafted them under Sarge's nose. Sarge did not respond.

Carmela snuck into the popemobile from the other side. She cut La-Trelle loose. Otto grinned at the two nuns. They smiled back, then simultaneously threw punches to each jaw. Teeth flew out of Otto's mouth as he dropped to the floor in a heap.

Not knowing LaTrelle was loose, Julius keep shooting arrows, knocking guns from the soldiers' hands. He sliced more than a few knuckles and hands, but none seriously.

LaTrelle pulled the knife from the sheath on her thigh and began to cut Nappy loose. Carmela threw her rosary around Adrian's neck and choked him from behind. Adrian grabbed at the rosary with both hands. As he let go of the steering wheel, the popemobile spun out of control, careened into the central altar and shattered it. The chapel shook. Columns cracked. Pieces of ceiling rained on the soldiers and popemobile.

"This better never happen to the Sistine Chapel," Julius mumbled as he shot another arrow.

Then Julius looked toward Adrian and saw Carmela choking him. He dropped the nun with the Vulcan nerve pinch. She slumped out of the popemobile as Adrian regained control of it. He turned the van around and drove down the chapel's main aisle.

Nappy's minions continued to try to get the van. Sister Angela sprang off a pew, grabbed the rack atop the popemobile and swung herself in, kicking Damian into a wall. Julius used Angela's momentum against her and threw her out the other side of the van. She slammed into a group of soldiers, knocking them down, as LaTrelle rolled out of the van with a groggy Nappy.

Julius saw them out of the corner of his eye. "Damn it. Let's get them!"

More chunks of ceiling fell. They blocked the popemobile from getting to Nappy and LaTrelle. Adrian backed up, trying to get around the soldiers and debris.

Nappy drooled on LaTrelle's shoulder and slumped against the confessional. He mumbled incoherently. "Bless me, Father, for I have sinned. My last confession was over twenty years ago."

"I hate to do this, but you need the antidote," LaTrelle said.

She kissed his mouth, then wiped her lips on her sleeve. With a shake of his head, Nappy began to snap out of his stupor. Chunks of brick and dust fell around them. Tires squealed and guns fired in the background.

"What's going on? Where's the tiara?" Nappy asked.

"We're under attack," LaTrelle said. "The chapel is collapsing."

"We have to get the tiara and get out," Nappy said wide-eyed.

"*Le Pape* is here," LaTrelle reminded him.

Nappy yawned. "Here?" He shook his head again. "I forgot about that."

"It's perfect," LaTrelle said. "Remember the prophecy. We can get *le Pape* to follow us and fulfill the prophecy."

"*Oui? Oui!*" Nappy agreed, as he finally comprehended.

LaTrelle stood and pulled the arm of a Mother Mary statue. The arm dropped. Part of the wall slid open as if rolling a stone to open a tomb, and a dimly lit secret passageway was revealed. As Nappy struggled to his feet an arrow pinned the collars of his shirt and coat to the confessional.

LaTrelle looked toward Julius, shocked. "Does he always have that bow with him?" she asked contemptuously. "He'll have his horse next."

Four more arrows in rapid succession pinned Nappy's arms. Then, under Sister Marie's direction, two soldiers began to set up a small cannon between the popemobile and LaTrelle and Nappy.

"That's not good," Adrian said.

Adrian tried to drive the van out of the cannon's line of fire and intercept Nappy and LaTrelle when another large chunk fell from the ceiling in front of him. He high-centered the van on the rubble.

"Sisters, this way!" LaTrelle called to Carmela, Angela and Marie.

The nuns ran toward LaTrelle and the passageway.

"Crap," Julius said.

Julius ripped off his cassock. He jumped out of the van wearing shorts, a cut-off Popeye T-shirt and sandals. He walked defiantly toward the cannon as he tugged off the goatee.

One of the soldiers recognized Julius and said, "*Le Pape?*"

The two soldiers look at each other befuddled.

The other soldier asked, "We've been shooting at *le Pape?*"

Julius nocked an arrow and aimed toward the cannon. The soldiers looked at each other again.

"Now *le Pape* will shoot at us!" the first soldier bellowed.

The soldiers crossed themselves and bowed their heads to receive their punishment. Julius shot an arrow into the barrel of the cannon and jammed it.

As LaTrelle reached to free Nappy from Julius' arrows, she glanced over her shoulder at Julius. Julius smiled at LaTrelle and mimicked her licking a dart. He put an arrowhead in his mouth, nocked the arrow and quickly shot. The arrow's broadhead grazed LaTrelle's cheek. Her eyes squinted. A trickle of blood flowed from her cheek. The arrow pinned her sleeve. A second arrow held her arm.

Sister Angela ran forward and snapped off the arrows holding LaTrelle. Carmela and Marie broke loose Nappy's arrows. With chunks and dust falling from the ceiling, Julius could not get another clear shot. He lowered his bow and ran toward them, dodging falling debris as he skittered through the rubble.

LaTrelle, Nappy and the other three nuns ran through the secret passageway to four scooters parked there. Their cornettes bounced into each other.

"Make your blowguns!" LaTrelle ordered.

Each nun fashioned a blowgun from her cornette and got on a scooter. LaTrelle and Nappy got on the same one. LaTrelle drove as Nappy held her by the waist. The tunnel door slammed shut just as Julius got there.

The popemobile finally spun its way off its high center, smashed into the small cannon as the soldiers dove out of its way. Adrian pulled up to Julius. Julius pulled the statue's arm to open the tunnel door. The van was too big to get through.

Julius whistled.

Outside in the palace courtyard, Eli waited patiently. His ears perked up when he heard Julius' whistle. He nibbled on a door handle, opened the door and loped into the palace.

With Nappy and the nuns now gone, Nappy's soldiers lowered their weapons and stopped their attack. Several expressed their feelings, to the agreement of all.

"Thank God he's gone."

"I thought he'd never leave."

"Good riddance."

"We haven't been paid in months."

"Like his great-great-great-great-great grandfather, he is."

"We are at your command, Your Holiness."

Otto began to regain consciousness as Adrian gave him smelling salts. Sarge blinked awake as Julius poured holy water on his head.

When Sarge seemed barely coherent, Julius said, "Sarge, take charge."

Eli ran to Julius. Julius swung upon him.

"I'll go after Nappy," he said. "Find and search his quarters for the tiara."

Eli reared and neighed.

"We'll meet later," Julius said, and galloped Eli into the tunnel.

The nuns and Nappy scooted toward the light at the end of the tunnel.

"Is he back there?" Nappy anxiously asked LaTrelle.

"He must be. I hear hoof beats," she answered.

"I have to get the tiara," Nappy said desperately.

LaTrelle radioed Sister Susan in the monitoring center. "Bring the tiara to the heliport. Quickly!" she said.

"*Oui!*" Susan replied. She dashed from her post and onto a scooter.

Nappy looked over his shoulder. "He's gaining on us!" he screamed into LaTrelle's ear.

"Don't do that," LaTrelle said. Then to the nuns behind her, she said, "Dart him!"

The sisters removed pins from their wind blown hair and put them in their mouths. They raised the guns toward Nappy.

"Not him!" LaTrelle admonished. "Him!" She pointed back to Julius.

The nuns turned and blew their guns. Darts came out of the dim light at Julius and Eli. Eli swerved. Julius ducked. The darts missed.

Led by one of Nappy's soldiers, Sarge, Adrian, Damian and Otto ran through a narrow hall to Nappy's quarters.

"In here," the soldier said.

As they opened the door, Susan raced out on a scooter with a backpack. She blow darted Sarge. Sarge slapped his neck.

"Bitch!" Sarge growled as he dropped unconscious into Damian's arms.

Otto swung up on the scooter and grabbed Susan from behind as she drove by. Grinning, he had a nun's breast in each hand. Susan elbowed him in the head and knocked him off. He tumbled along the floor.

"Aaaiieeeeeeeeeeeeee!" Otto wailed.

The four scooters exited the tunnel and pulled up to the heliport. Nappy's helicopter hovered slightly and noisily above the ground. A soldier pulled Nappy inside. Susan rode up with the backpack. Stretching, she handed it up to Nappy.

Julius and Eli galloped from the tunnel and toward the helicopter, fifty meters away. Guiding Eli with his knees, Julius nocked and fired an arrow. It nipped Nappy's hand.

"Yeow!" Nappy howled.

He dropped the backpack.

LaTrelle caught it. She waved the nuns onto the helicopter. They scrambled aboard, then LaTrelle got on.

As the helicopter lifted, Julius reached the helicopter, stood atop the saddle and grabbed at one of the helicopter's landing skids. He just missed it.

LaTrelle looked down at Julius from the helicopter doorway. Julius looked up at her. The rotor wash from the helicopter engulfed them as it hovered for a moment.

"*Que sera sera*," LaTrelle said somewhat regretfully.

Julius read her lips and replied, "*Que sera sera.*"

A drop of blood fell from LaTrelle's cheek and splattered onto Julius'. LaTrelle saw it land, then she looked into Julius' eyes. She touched her cheek where Julius' arrow nicked her.

Sister Susan touched LaTrelle's shoulder from behind. LaTrelle turned toward her.

"Sit down, Sister," Susan said sympathetically.

LaTrelle discreetly waved at Julius, then turned out of the doorway of the helicopter as it flew off.

Julius slid into his saddle and watched the helicopter disappear into the sunset. The rotor wash ruffled his hair and Eli's mane. He dabbed the drop of blood from his cheek with a white handkerchief. Emotionless, he turned Eli and rode away.

Adrian and Damian checked Nappy's quarters for clues about the tiara. Damian went through a closet. Adrian searched a chest and bureau. Sarge lay unconscious on the couch. A scraped and bruised Otto sagged in a chair.

Julius rode up and walked inside. The men look at him questioningly.

"I didn't get it," Julius said flatly. "Find anything?"

Adrian pointed to a hat stand. "The tiara was here. We just missed the sister who rode out with it."

Otto pushed himself up painfully in the chair. "I just missed it," he said defiantly.

"Want to go home?" Julius asked Otto.

"Not until I get my hands on that nun again," Otto said with conviction.

Julius looked at Sarge. "Did he have a relapse?"

"He got darted again," Adrian explained.

Julius looked into Sarge's face. "That can't be good," he pronounced.

Julius turned to Nappy's soldier. "Any idea where Nappy would go?"

"No, Your Holiness," the soldier replied. "He only confided in the sisters."

"Thank you," Julius said. "You can leave."

The soldier saluted and left.

"I found something," Adrian said.

Julius walked to Nappy's desk where Adrian sat with an old, yellowish parchment. A portrait of Napoleon Bonaparte wearing a Hooters ball cap hung on the wall behind the desk.

"This seems to be some sort of ancient prophecy," Adrian said. "It's in Greek. The wax stamp shows it to be from the Vatican Archives. I wonder how Nappy got it."

"Probably from the real Napoleon," Julius surmised. "I doubt everything he stole was returned to the Vatican after Waterloo. I guess you could say it was Waterlooted."

"Care to take a look?" Adrian asked, referring to the parchment.

Julius replied, "Go ahead. Your Greek is better than mine."

"Here's what I get," Adrian began. "When Heaven's Crown is lost, the Iconoclast will be driven from Babylon across the water to a False Oasis where water rises upon the desert and Jezebels rule its throne at night. There, supplicants suckle at a great city's teats, and abecedarians wage lots for its favor."

"What's an abecedarian?" Julius asked.

"A beginner," Adrian explained.

Julius nodded. "Thanks. Continue."

Adrian studied the prophecy a bit longer, then said, "Beneath Heaven's Wrath, the multitude will be driven before the Lost Tribes of Israel and a syzygy will appear within The Forbidden Temple, heralding the exchange of Heaven's Crown through the hands of The Trinity."

"What's a syzygy?" Julius asked.

"An alignment of three heavenly bodies, such as the sun, the earth and the full moon."

"Really? OK. Go ahead," Julius said.

Adrian continued. "There, where iniquity is witnessed by antiquity, the Iconoclast must come under the watch of false gods to break the vow that sets him apart from men and women. But if the Heavens do not yield the Crown to the True Ruler to reconcile secular and spiritual, temporal will overcome Divine, and the Promised Peace of the syzygy will be extinguished forever."

Adrian looked up from the prophecy.

"That's some heavy shit," Damian concluded.

Julius pensively walked around the room.

"Is it real?" Adrian asked.

"I hear rumors of such a prophecy," Julius said thoughtfully.

"Why can't Nappy wear the tiara?" Damian asked.

"Julius II was a huge practical joker, and a favorite among the witches and charmers who worked at The Vatican. Near the end of his life, he had a spell put on his tiara so only a celibate pope could wear it," Julius replied.

"I bet that cut down on the popes who could wear it," Adrian reasoned.

"It did," Julius agreed. "Quite the legacy from a man who said the only Holy Trinity worth getting on his knees for was a *ménage à trois*."

Otto's eyes got wide at hearing that. He stirred in the chair.

Adrian thought for a moment, and then said, "Without such a spell, almost anyone could fulfill this prophecy."

"Then why did Nappy take it?" Damian asked.

"To crown himself pope," Julius said simply.

"Can he do that?" Damian asked.

"Technically, yes. Any Catholic man can become pope," Julius said.

"But if he can't wear it ..." Damian wondered aloud.

"Unless the prophecy is fulfilled," Adrian explained.

"At the right time and place," added Julius.

"So Nappy is the True Ruler?" Damian asked.

Julius shrugged. "He seems to think so."

"Oh," Damian conceded.

Adrian scanned the prophecy again, then turned to Julius. "Any idea where the False Oasis is?"

Julius picked up Las Vegas tourist info from Nappy's desk. "There's only one place besides the Vatican that twisted."

He dropped a brochure in front of Adrian. It featured what was billed as Las Vegas' newest resort and casino ~ The Basilica.

"Las Vegas," Adrian concluded.

"It's our only lead," Julius agreed.

Damian shook Sarge. "Sarge, wake up! We're going to Vegas."

Otto sat back, grinned and rubbed himself. "I'm getting some lumber."

Chapter XII

City in the Desert

NAPPY AND LATRELLE sat at a window table at the Las Vegas Eiffel Tower Restaurant. It was mid afternoon; the restaurant was less than half occupied.

Nappy sneezed, then sipped his wine and said, "Before I can wear the tiara and claim the papacy, *le Pape* has to lose his celibacy."

"Easy for you to say," LaTrelle said, as she gazed across The Strip to the Bellagio.

"I vow to become pope. You are who must take Julius' virtue from him."

LaTrelle poked at her salad with a fork. "You think it will be easy? His morals – and his body – are rock solid."

Nappy slurped his soup and patted his mouth with a napkin. "Be positive," he said. "You will get what you want out of this, too."

"If the convent wasn't closing and I wasn't charged with taking care of my sisters, I would not do it," LaTrelle said with an edge in her voice.

Nappy smiled and sipped his wine. "See? We're all working towards the greater good."

LaTrelle was mildly combative. "Are you sure your interpretations of the prophecy are correct?"

"My great-great-great-great-great grandfather would not have kept it in his personal safe otherwise," Nappy said placidly. "I've had years to work with experts to decipher its meaning."

Nappy reached in a vest pocket of his Napoleonic coat and unfolded a copy of the prophecy. He glanced at it briefly, then looked up and said, "The prophecy states the Iconoclast, that is, Julius – who attacks the beliefs of his own church – will be forced to leave Babylon. Rome has been referred to as Babylon for centuries. We forced Julius out when we reclaimed the tiara. And we tracked his plane across the water, across the Atlantic. Soon he'll land in Vegas, at the threshold of the Forbidden Temple. That is where you will break his vow of ..."

"Celibacy," LaTrelle added flatly.

"*Oui*!" Nappy agreed happily. "I know Julius. There's no other vow he's kept; and no other vow he wants to break. You'll do him a favor, LaTrelle. As the prophecy states, it's what sets him apart from men and women."

LaTrelle glanced out the window again. "Where is this Forbidden Temple?" she asked.

Nappy sneezed and blew his nose. "We shall go there after lunch."

"Will he be able to find it?" LaTrelle asked, referring to Julius. "The bible is loaded with cities in the desert."

"With the clues I left at the palace, you'd have to be an idiot to miss it," Nappy said confidently.

"So will he be able to find it?" she asked again.

"*Oui*. Vegas has a thousand times the infamy of Sodom and Gomorrah. Look around." Nappy waved a hand. "A restaurant in the Eiffel Tower in Las Vegas, Nevada, USA? How could he not find The Basilica and Forbidden Temple?

LaTrelle put some spread on a cracker. "I suppose," she said, took a bite and chewed. "By the way, the equine pate' is very good."

Chapter XIII

Dogfight

JULIUS, ADRIAN, DAMIAN and Otto were aboard the papal Lear. Sarge, the co-pilot, sat next to Gino, the pilot. Eli was corralled in the back by cargo netting.

Otto clutched a Vegas showgirl brochure to his chest.

"Get away. It's mine," he said hostilely to Damian.

"C'mon. Let me see it," Damian laughed.

Gino played a video game on one of the cockpit's video screens. After a bit, he looked down and out the window, then spoke into the microphone.

"Prepare for landing," he said. "We're approaching McCarran International Airport. Strange, though, I don't remember Lake Mead looking this big from the air."

Gino looked at his controls. "Uh-oh. We're way off course. I should know better than to fly when I play this thing."

He hurriedly shut down the game and took control.

"The tower has cleared us for landing," Sarge said.

"Really? From where?" Gino asked incredulously.

Sarge touched his headset to listen more closely. "From the Spanish I'd say Havana, Cuba."

Jets appeared on either side of the cockpit. Their pilots turned their thumbs upside down, signaling the Lear to land.

"Holy shit! Cuban MiGs!" Gino hollered.

Gino put the Lear into a vertical climb, pinning everyone to the back of his seat.

"Woo-hoo!" Otto shouted gleefully.

The putti, grabbed the arms of their "seats," and tilted backward helplessly in the air near the pope.

"Whoa!" they exclaimed.

The MiG pilots looked at each other and gave chase. They were quickly on the tail of the Lear, as it climbed toward a column of clouds. The red putto grabbed an airsick bag and vomited.

Oxygen masks dropped. Julius slid past the puking putto and hurried toward the back of the plane. He put an oxygen mask on Eli and one on himself, and stayed near Eli.

The Lear made it into partial cloud cover as MiG tracer shells ripped into the cabin. Eli lifted his tail and crapped. Horseshit was sucked through some of the bullet holes in the fuselage.

One MiG pilot saw the horseshit coming, but could not avoid it. It splattered into the windshield. The pilot looked in horror as a crucifix-shaped crack spread out from a divot in the windshield. The crack quickly grew before the pilot's eyes. The windshield gave way and shattered into the cockpit, spraying the pilot with shit and glass. He ejected and the MiG tumbled toward the sea.

The second MiG fired a missile. The Lear pilot deployed flares. The missile hit the flare and exploded harmlessly as the Lear continued to weave up through the clouds.

"We're almost out of their airspace!" the pilot hollered as he glanced at his locator panel.

The Lear stalled. The MiG screamed past it through the clouds, barely avoiding a collision. The men inside watched through the windows as it flashed by. The Lear began to drop out of the sky as the pilot tried to restart its engines. As the MiG circled back for the kill, the Lear's engines fired. The pilot nosed the plane into a vertical dive. The red putto kept vomiting. Eli and Julius slid against the cargo netting while the other men lunged forward.

"For God's sakes, Gino, land!" Sarge implored.

"No way I'm dying in a Cuban shit hole," Gino said.

"We don't have a chance!" Sarge hollered.

"MiGs don't fly well at sea level. The air's too dense. It might crash."

A radar operator at Florida's Tyndall Air Force Base checked blips on the radar screen. He turned to the colonel.

"We may have a defector, sir," he said. "A MiG is heading northwest at Mach 0.84. There's another blip on the screen with a Lear Jet's signature."

The colonel leaned toward the screen to look for himself. "Castro must be defecting in style," he mused.

"If that's true, then his Lear is under attack," the operator said.

"How close are they to our airspace?" the colonel asked, now more interested.

"They're on a bearing for Disney World, sir," came the reply.

"So much for normalized relations," the colonel said, then he barked into a microphone, "Scramble the F-16s."

Two pilots raced from the cafeteria to their fighter jets. They were in the air and on course for the Lear in less than a minute.

The Lear screamed low over the ocean with the MiG on its tail. Gino checked his radar warning receiver.

"We're screwed. He's a C-hair away from missile lock," he said drily.

Adrian worked his calculator. "The odds of surviving a crash in the water at almost 600 mph is ..."

Sarge looked over his shoulder at Adrian. "Save it for Vegas!"

The MiG pilot's finger rested on the missile launch button. His launch platform's illuminator radar lit up. He fired.

As the missile was about to hit the Lear, a whale spouted between the two jets. The spray threw the missile slightly off course, but it exploded near the Lear. Shrapnel cut into the fuselage.

Julius spun around as shrapnel ripped his shirt, immediately soaking it in blood. He was hit in the shoulder and chest. His bow, quiver and arrows were shredded. He slumped into Eli, who was not hit. Eli lay down with Julius at his midsection. Julius touched Eli's head.

"We'll get out of this," he said weakly and smiled.

As the MiG was about to finish off the Lear with its cannon, an F-16 attacked it from above. Tracer shells ripped the MiG's fuselage and nose. The MiG banked sharply and headed south. The F-16s chased it briefly, but stopped when they were near Cuban air space.

"Break off the attack," the flight commander said. "Let's look for the Lear. It's not showing on radar."

The pilots scanned the ocean, flying at about 200 meters. After making several passes over the dogfight area, the commander called an end to the search.

"Must've been a clean hit," he said. "Return to base. We'll leave the rest up to the Navy."

The F-16s banked toward the north and headed back to their base. Meanwhile, the Lear still flew low across the water.

"We're going down," Gino said.

"Are we hit?" Sarge asked nervously.

"Well, yeah, but we're also 1,000 miles off course. We're out of fuel," Gino answered. "Everyone assume the crash position."

A few moments later, the plane skipped several times on the surface of the Gulf of Mexico, then stopped. Julius rested against Eli. Pale and bleeding, he stroked Eli as the two looked into each other's eyes, then Julius closed his eyes and let his head fall. Eli whinnied softly.

The white putto mopped the red putto's vomit into a bucket, which hung in the air. The red putto floated on his back.

"The next pope better be a pussy," the white putto said. "I'm not doing this again."

Some distance away, the crew of The Apocalypse, a fishing yacht, saw the Lear skip on the waves. Peter, the elderly skipper watched closely. With gray and dark brown hair and beard, he looked exactly like the man being crucified upside down in the chapel painting to whom Julius had prayed. Peter wore white shorts and a green T-shirt that read, "Fish, it's what's for dinner."

"Let's get 'em, boys!" Peter said, as the Lear rested on the water.

Inside the Lear, the men unbuckled their seats belts, amazed to be alive.

"Helluva landing!" said Damian.

"Great job!" commended Sarge.

"Woo-hoo!" Otto raved.

"What are the odds?" asked Adrian.

"Playing those crash landing video games paid off after all," Gino said, smiling.

"Now what?" Sarge asked.

Gino pushed buttons and clicked switches. "We have about five minutes until the plane sinks." He turned to Sarge. "Release the lifeboat out of the back."

"10-4," Sarge said and got up to go to the back of the plane.

Engines on the plane's sides disengaged, moved on tracks under the wings, elongated and turned into pontoons. A smaller pontoon held up the nose.

Otto looked out over the ocean. "It's a miracle," he proclaimed.

"It's technology," Adrian corrected.

Sarge saw Eli lying down and realized he did not see Julius. He hurried over to Eli and found Julius, unconscious and bleeding, at Eli's midsection.

"The pope's hit!" he hollered. "He looks bad."

With Peter at the wheel, the yacht cruised at full speed and soon was along side the Lear.

The Lear's door opened.

"Ahoy!" Peter called. "Is everyone OK?"

Sarge appeared in the doorway. "We have the pope," he answered. "He's been shot."

"We'll take care of him," Peter called from the deck. Then he turned to his crew. "Matthew and Mark, prepare the boom. Andrew, get ready to bring them on deck. John, are you getting all this?"

John, apparently a man in his early thirties, looked through the eyepiece of a video camera. He had long, light brown hair and wore an untucked Hawaiian print shirt and surfer shorts. He was the only crewman without a beard.

"Yep," John replied. "This video camera I got for Christmas is much better than writing longhand. It's a Revelation."

Mark wore overalls and sat at the controls of a lift. He hoisted a gangplank to the Lear, connecting the two crafts. Adrian waited at the Lear's doorway and hooked the gangplank to the threshold. Damian came onto the gangplank with an unconscious Julius in his arms. Blood covered Julius' shirt and Damian's arms and hands. Damian carried the pope to the yacht.

"He looks worse than I thought he would," Peter said quietly to himself. Then he barked more orders. "Philip, take Damian and Julius to Luke in the infirmary. James, you and Jude prepare food and drinks for our guests. Thomas, find them something decent to wear. They smell like putti vomit. Judas, quit messing around with that rope and help Mark put the gangplank away."

Philip, wearing shorts and a T-shirt, led Damian below deck. James and Jude each wore a shortie wet suit. They followed Philip and Damian down the stairs.

A smiling Otto and Gino came across next. Adrian followed, and then Sarge lead Eli across the gangplank.

Peter looked admiringly at Eli. "That's a hell of a horse," he said. "Had the Lord ridden into Jerusalem on such an animal, instead of that ass, he never would have been crucified."

Eli nodded his head effusively.

Sarge walked up to Peter and extended his hand. "Thank you very much, sir. My name is Kaspar Von Soldaten. Everyone calls me Sarge."

The skipper took his hand. "I'm Peter. That's Matthew, Mark and John. You'll meet the other crewmen later."

The other guards and pilot came over and introduced themselves to the yachtsmen. They all shook hands.

"What about the pope?" Sarge asked.

"He'll be fine," Peter answered. "Now get yourselves cleaned up and have some refreshments."

Adrian whispered into Sarge's ear as they followed a couple of the yachtsmen below deck. "I think we've been saved by St. Peter and the Apostles."

"I hope so," Sarge answered, "because it'll take a miracle to save Julius."

A bearded, bespectacled Luke, wearing scrubs and surgical mask, worked on Julius. Peter came in to assist.

"How is he?" Peter asked.

"It's not like he was crucified," Luke replied, as he dropped bloody shrapnel from Julius into a basin, "but he lost a lot of blood. That I can replace with seawater, but his right shoulder and lung are pretty torn up."

"Once you get that shrapnel out, I'll work some magic on his chest," Peter said, "but I'm not good with shoulders. Are you?"

"I have an old remedy from the Spartans. Hand me two of those centaur ligaments, please," Luke said to Peter, as he nodded towards a jar.

On deck, the other men engaged in various tasks to pass the time. Damian arm wrestled Matthew. Otto looked at showgirl brochures with Judas. Adrian diagramed human evolution to a few others on a whiteboard. Sarge stayed with Eli and talked to Mark. Gino played video games with John.

Chapter XIV

The Basilica

NAPPY, IN NAPOLEONIC clothes and two-cornered hat, and Sister La-Trelle in traditional religious dress, walked The Strip after lunch. A happy Nappy pointed out landmarks that coincided with the prophecy he carried. They walked past the Bellagio. Its fountains erupted.

"A False Oasis where water will rise upon the desert ..." Nappy said wryly, referring to the prophecy.

"... and Jezebels rule its throne." LaTrelle added disdainfully as two hookers walked up to Nappy.

The girls, one brown and one white, wore short skirts, boots, tight blouses and a lot of make up.

The white girl looked at Nappy. "You're so cute," she cooed. "Love the outfit."

She slinked around Nappy. She let a finger barely touch and slide on his cheek.

Nappy smiled uneasily.

The brown girl looked him up and down and smiled. "What's your name?" she asked.

"Nappy. It's short for Napoleon."

"Love it!" the brown girl said, bouncing up and down.

She put her arm around the white girl and they wiggled their hips in front of Nappy. LaTrelle watched with her arms crossed.

"What's yours?" Nappy asked tentatively.

"What's my name or what's my line?" the brown girl laughed lightly.

"Your name," Nappy said slowly and befuddled.

"Cookie," answered the brown girl.

"Mine's Milk," added the white girl. "How about some Milk and Cookie?"

"And we can have a little Nappy-poo," Cookie chuckled.

A security guard walked over. "OK, ladies, you know the rules. No soliciting here until after dark."

The two girls laughed, jostled each other, waved good-bye and walked on. Nappy tentatively waved back.

He and LaTrelle continued down The Strip for about a quarter of a mile, then stopped at the bottom of the steps that lead to The Basilica. Fake columns supported the canopy in front of The Basilica, which resembled the famous cathedral.

"*Incroyable!*" LaTrelle pronounced.

"*Oui!*" Nappy affirmed.

He jogged buoyantly up the steps with LaTrelle along side. Young men in Vatican Guard uniforms were posted at the entryway. Each held a halberd. Two of them opened the door for Nappy and LaTrelle. They walked in and through the spacious lobby. Statues of saints surrounded its fountain. Biblical-theme paintings covered the walls, somehow resembling the work of great Renaissance masters.

The atmosphere changed as they entered the crowded lounge dominated by multi-colored neon lights. Teat City Brewery ™ neon signs flashed above bartenders and customers at the bar.

"Supplicants will suckle at a great city's teats ..." Nappy said happily, quoting another part of the prophecy.

He and LaTrelle passed players at banks of slot machines. Novice gamblers were at the tables, getting lessons from the dealers. Nappy looked smug.

"... and abecedarians wage lots for its favor," he observed blithely.

They followed signs to the elevators and swimming pools.

"Napoleon!" the security guard posted at the elevator said to Nappy. "Here to loot The Vatican again?"

Nappy's confidence quickly changed to confusion and nervousness.

"He's joking," LaTrelle assured him. Then she spoke to the guard. "Those days are over. He's here for some fun before going into exile."

The guard laughed. "Enjoy yourselves."

Nappy and LaTrelle got in an elevator. Nappy pushed the button for the Pool Level. The elevator went up and opened poolside to a late afternoon sun. People stared curiously at Nappy and LaTrelle as they stepped out.

The pools and bars were crowded. Palm trees and awnings provided some shade. Sculptures of gods abounded, as well as lions, mermaids and eagles.

Nappy and LaTrelle walked across a bridge over a pool. They stopped in front of a large placard. It read: "Tonight only! Jason and The Lost Tribes of Israel play poolside at The Basilica."

Nappy was again ecstatic. He squeezed LaTrelle's arm. "You see? The Lost Tribes of Israel. And with the full moon, tonight is the night of the syzygy. Sister LaTrelle Terre, you are the earth. Pope Julius Sole' is the sun. You, Julius and the moon are the prophecy's Trinity, a replica of the tiara's top three jewels, and why the time is now. When you mount him, you three must be in perfect alignment.

LaTrelle shook her head. They continued to stroll through the crowd and toward another pool.

"*Mon Dieu,*" LaTrelle lamented. "Look at all these people."

"Only the gods will see you," Nappy comforted.

"*Impossible,*" LaTrelle replied.

Nappy smiled uncontrollably. "Oh, no. Not with that." He pointed to a secluded light blue cabana in the trees. "*La pièce de résistance* ~ The Forbidden Temple."

A sign in front of it read "The Forbidden Temple ~ Reserved".

"The cabana?" LaTrelle asked.

"*Oui*. That is where you will take Julius. I reserved it for twenty-four hours, not that you will need that long," he smiled.

"*Incroyable*," LaTrelle said softly.

"It's all in the prophecy," Nappy affirmed. "Get the other sisters and get ready. We will meet at my hotel room at 10 o'clock. I'll have the tiara."

"You'll bring the tiara here?" she asked.

"Of course. I can't wait to see the look in Julius' eyes when I put it on. Then I'll have it all: empire, the papacy and the tiara. Julius can keep his horse," Nappy said derisively.

LaTrelle looked around. She took in an expansive view to the north and west. Thunderheads were building over the mountains.

Chapter XV

Transfiguration

JULIUS AWOKE AND sat up in bed. He wore pajama bottoms. His upper body was wrapped in bandages. His right arm was in a sling. He didn't quite feel like getting up yet. He took a deck of cards and a tray off the bedside table. He slowly shuffled and started to play solitaire to clear his head.

Soon, a smiling St. Peter walked into the cabin. "How do you feel?" he asked happily.

"Peter!" Julius said with surprise and delight. He put all the cards down on the tray. "I should have known you were behind this. I haven't seen you since soon after I became pope."

"After I introduce myself to a new pontiff, I try to stay out of the way," Peter said, "but your case has always been a little different."

"So where are we now?" Julius asked.

"My yacht," Peter answered.

"Nice boat," Julius said.

"The last 2,000 years have been good to me," Peter conceded, "although the fishing isn't what it used to be."

"Fill me in on more recent times. I remember getting hit in the plane, but little else until I woke up here. What happened? How are my men? How long have I been out?" Julius asked.

"Despite his error, your pilot did an amazing job landing the Lear on the ocean after American fighter planes drove off the MiG. We happened to be in the area ..."

"Happened to be in the area," Julius chuckled. "I like that."

"We happened to be in the area, saw your plane come down, and knew you'd need help. Your other men are OK, but you were a mess. Luke took care of you."

"Luke the Evangelist or M.D?" Julius asked.

"Same difference," said Peter.

"Wow," Julius said softly, paused, then added, "I really appreciate this, Peter."

"You've been aboard about two hours. We don't have a lot of extra time now, so I need to be direct. You're going to Vegas?" Peter asked.

"I am."

Peter looked deeply into Julius' eyes. "You know it's a trap," he said.

"I do."

"I mean the tiara is a trap," Peter explained.

"Yep, known it all along."

"You could get your nuts in a vice," Peter cautioned.

"That would make celibacy easier."

"Celibacy is an option, not a command," Peter said.

"I know. My father was pope."

"You can change that option officially, if you want." Peter suggested.

"I need to get the tiara first."

Peter shook his head. "Let's have a look at you," he said.

Peter cradled Julius' right arm, removed it from the sling, and then began to unwrap Julius' bandages. He tossed a wad of white gauze into a wastebasket and said, "Nappy is no joke. This prophecy is real."

Julius paid scant attention to Peter as he looked at his exposed upper body. "No scabs. No scars," he said appreciatively.

"And no stigmata," Peter added.

Peter stretched and massaged Julius' right arm and shoulder. "I'm not sure if you truly comprehend what's going on with this prophecy. Do not underestimate Sister LaTrelle. If you do, Nappy can become pope, the Earth may be consumed by fire, and humanity's conscious evolution will be delayed at least twenty-five thousand years."

"Am I on a quest or a guilt trip?" Julius asked bemused.

Peter shrugged. "Sorry. Old habits die hard."

He lowered Julius' arm and pulled up a chair next to the bed. "Do you want to be known as a serious pope or a freak?" Peter asked.

"What's the difference?"

"Very little," Peter acknowledged.

"That's what I thought."

"Let me put it this way," Peter said with a hint of frustration. "I heard your prayer in the chapel. If you want to set things straight, fulfill the prophecy."

"I'm not sure what it means," Julius said honestly.

"Well, don't ask me," Peter said. "I was the thick headed apostle. That's why Christ could build his Church on me."

Recalling his prayer in the chapel, Julius flexed his arm and moved his shoulder as he asked, "Were you really crucified upside down?"

Peter crossed his fingers behind his back and said, "Figure out the prophecy and maybe I'll tell you."

Peter got up. He walked to a locker and got a sleek wooden recurve bow and quiver of arrows. He held the bow out to Julius.

"Here," he said. "Yours was shot up by a MiG."

Julius stood up as Peter handed him the bow.

"The Bow of the Covenant!" Julius gasped, turning the weapon about as he examined it.

"You're deranged," Peter said. "It's special, but not that special. Luke put something extra into your shoulder. You should be able to shoot it."

Julius braced one tip of the bow against his foot and strung the bow with ease. He nocked an arrow and quickly shot through a port side porthole. The arrow flew over the ocean. It cleanly split a fish in the beaks of two gulls fighting a tug-of-war over it in the air. Each gull flew off with half a fish.

"My shoulder feels great!" Julius exclaimed.

Peter was pleased. "Excellent! The saints can help, but can't interfere," he said. "Let's go on deck. You need to get to Vegas tonight."

The shrapnel removed from Julius was in a bottle on a table by the bed. As Julius left, he put the bottle and other personal items in a pajama pocket, and a medal around his neck.

Julius and Peter went up the stairs and walked on deck. Julius had the bow and arrows. Sarge, Adrian, Damian and Gino hurried over. Otto shuffled. Sarge and Julius hugged.

"We thought we lost you," a teary-eyed Sarge said.

"I'm fine, Sarge," Julius assured with a smile.

Peter interrupted. "No time to dawdle. Eli, come here."

Eli trotted over to Peter. Peter stroked Eli's muzzle.

"The bible says the Lord will return when horses fly," Peter said.

"Actually, I wrote that," John said.

"In any case, Eli," Peter continued, "wings will help you fit in in Vegas."

In a flash of light, Eli had a Pegasus-like transformation. His shimmering gold coat was now almost white. He fanned his wings, pranced and nodded his head effusively. The sight transfixed the men.

"This is quite some help, Peter," Julius mused.

"It's easier than raising the Lear from the bottom of the ocean," Peter explained. "I'm not Yoda, you know. Now, for you."

In another flash of light, Julius' pajamas were replaced with black pants and a flowing white shirt.

Julius appraised his look. "I like it!" he said.

Julius swung up on Eli. He put the bow and quiver into a scabbard on Eli's side. Peter handed him sunglasses.

"Eli, take him to Vegas," Peter commanded. To Julius he said, "You're on your own. The others will follow. Fulfill the prophecy. Get the tiara. Save the papacy. Oh, and have fun."

Eli beat his wings slowly, took flight and circled the yacht. Peter looked up. The others watched in amazement.

"Julius," Peter called.

Julius whirled around on Eli.

"Don't turn your back on LaTrelle," Peter warned. "She can change everything."

"She already has," Julius said.

Eli reared and pawed his forelegs in the air. Julius waved. They turned and flew northwest.

"What are his odds?" Adrian asked Peter.

Peter kept his eyes to the sky. "God only knows and She's not telling me," he replied. Then he smiled at Adrian and looked to the other men. "To Lake Bellagio!" he ordered.

Julius and Eli disappeared over the cloudless sea. The yacht cruised in the same direction.

At dusk, purple and pink clouds speckled the sky over the Mojave Desert. Eli and Julius flew over mountains, canyons, mesas, cacti and shrubs basking in the fading light. The lights of Las Vegas glowed faintly in the distance.

From his airborne vantage point, Julius saw what he was looking for. "Let's stop at that water hole, Eli," he said. "I don't want you drinking from the fountains in Vegas."

They glided down and landed near a young, longhaired couple having sex by some car-sized boulders and Joshua trees near the water hole. They did not see each other until Eli and Julius were almost on top of the couple.

The woman was on her back ; the man was on top of her. She opened her eyes and saw Eli and Julius as they were about to land.

"Jesus Christ!" the woman said, pushing the man off of her.

"Nope, just the pope," Julius comforted. "Sorry about the *coitus interruptus*. My horse needs a drink."

The startled naked couple stood up, mostly blocked from Julius' view by a large rock. Julius dismounted and stretched. Eli began to drink.

"Holy shit! It is the pope," the young man declared.

The woman punished him with an elbow in the ribs.

"Ow! You're all over the news," he reported. "Said your plane went down in the Gulf."

"It did," Julius said.

He dipped his face and drank from a water pocket atop a boulder.

"I think we're supposed to kiss his ring or something," the woman said to the man.

She came out from behind a boulder. Her very long hair covered her breasts. She knelt at Julius' groin.

"Under the circumstances, that's not necessary," Julius said. He helped her up.

Pulling on a pair of shorts, the man walked over. "The pope. This is so trippy!" he exclaimed.

The woman turned toward Eli. "Your horse is magnificent."

"We didn't hear you ride in," the young man added. "It's like you dropped out of the sky."

Eli walked over as he fanned his wings.

"Oh ... my ... God! This is so trippy!" the main said again, slapping himself in the head. "A fucking, flying horse!"

Julius smiled. "Eli is a trip. I'm Julius."

The young man shook Julius' outstretched hand. "Hello, Your Holiest. I'm Jason and this is my wife, Patti."

Patti curtsied, then jumped up and down and clapped. "Oh, Father Pope Holiest, can we get a couple of selfies with you?" she asked excitedly.

"That'd be so cool," Jason agreed. "Otherwise, my mom won't believe we met you while banging in the desert. She's wild, crazy, sexy for you."

"Sure," Julius said.

"You look like Lady Godiva," Julius observed. "Why don't you hop up on Eli and Jason can take your picture."

"Oh ... my ... God," Jason said. "We could use that on our next flyer, Patti."

Patti got on Eli as Jason quickly set up his camera on a tripod. The desert lighting was perfect as Jason snapped pictures of Patti. In several shots, Eli demurely covered parts of Patti with his wings. After Jason and Patti got fully clothed, Jason put his camera on timer and took several pictures of them all together.

Jason offered Julius a joint. He took a hit and passed it to Patti.

"How can we get you these selfies?" she asked.

Julius handed her a card from his wallet. "Here's my email address," he said.

Jason slapped his head. "The pope's email address. This is so bitchin'!"

Julius smiled. "And I have something for you," he said.

Julius reached into a shirt pocket and unwrapped a rosary from his white handkerchief. He noticed the spot of LaTrelle's blood on it. Like the tattoo on LaTrelle's thigh, it was in the shape of a small, red heart. He studied it for a moment, then turned to Patti.

"For you, my personal rosary," he said.

Patti jumped up and down, curtsied, hugged Julius and happily took his rosary. "Thank you, Your Holiest."

Next, Julius took a medal from his neck and put it around Jason's. "Jason, here's a medal of Anthony the Great, Patron Saint of the Desert." Julius looked at the sky. "I have to go now. I have a date in Vegas."

"We do, too," Jason said. "Our band has a gig there tonight. We may have missed it if you hadn't dropped in."

"Will you bless us before you go, Father Pope Holiest?" Patti asked.

Julius smiled. "Of course."

Jason and Patti knelt. They botched crossing themselves as Julius put his hands on their heads and blessed them. Julius smiled.

As the couple stood up, Julius said, "I really do have to go."

Julius checked Eli, secured his few belongings and swung up on his horse. The western sky filled more with ominous clouds. Thunder rumbled. A breeze blew dust and plant debris across the ground. Trees rustled. A full moon was just beginning to rise on the eastern horizon.

"Peace, my friends," Julius said as he flashed the peace sign.

"We love you, Your Holiest," Patti beamed.

"Maybe we'll see you on The Strip," Jason added.

As Eli rose into the sky, Julius looked down and saw Jason and Patti pick up their blanket and gear, and run to their van. *Jason and the Lost Tribes of Israel* ™ was painted on the side of their van.

Chapter XVI

Syzygy

ELI AND JULIUS quickly flew toward Las Vegas. The blue light from the Luxor pyramid guided them. Soon, the light of the moon faded above the lights of the city. The desert storm to the west built with sporadic lightning and thunder.

Eli and Julius circled down slowly towards The Strip, viewing all things Vegas. A few helicopters carried tourists over the city for a nighttime view. Julius saw a distinctive dome reminiscent of a large cathedral.

"There's The Basilica, Eli," he said and guided them toward it.

As they dropped from the sky, people on the street looked up at them.

"Look. Up in the sky!" said the Elvis Impersonator.

"It's a bird!" said Batman.

"It's a plane!" said a jogger.

"It's a man on a flying horse!" Superman proclaimed, standing vigilantly with his hands on his hips.

A small child tugged on her father's hand. "Daddy, can we get tickets to fly on the horse?" she asked.

Her father looked down at her. "We'll see, honey. I'm not sure where to get them."

Next to them a street vendor held up a roll of tickets and hawked, "Get your tickets here to ride the Flying Wonder Horse."

People again stopped and stared as Sisters LaTrelle, Susan, Carmela, Angela and Marie walked through The Basilica. They wore traditional cornettes and nontraditional miniskirts. Nappy carried the tiara in a hatbox. He sneezed occasionally.

They walked through the bar and casino to the elevators. The security guard posted at the elevator smiled at them as they approached.

"The Duke of Wellington is waiting for you poolside, Your Excellency," he said, pressing the elevator "Up" button for them.

Nappy gripped the hatbox tightly. "What?" he said fearfully.

"He's joking again," LaTrelle said.

The guard smiled at the nuns and held open the elevator door. The six quickly walked inside.

"I don't like that man," Nappy said as the elevator began to rise.

"Did you read his nametag?" LaTrelle asked, smiling. "It said 'Duke.'"

Nappy and the nuns exited the elevator and went to the crowded poolside. It was a warm, desert evening. A soulful blues song blared from the PA system. Palm trees and other vegetation swayed in the breeze.

Nappy looked around as they walked. "He'll be here soon. We must get settled."

"I don't see any open tables," LaTrelle said.

A Basilica security guard noticed them and came over to help.

"Good evening, Sisters and sir," he said. "Where would you like to sit?"

"A table by the Forbidden Temple would be perfect," Nappy said brusquely.

"Follow me," the guard said and walked with them past people, trees, fountains and statues to a table on a pool overlook near the Forbidden

Temple cabana. The table was partially secluded from the rest of the area. Several young men sat there with their drinks.

"Gentlemen, would you be so kind as to give your table to the sisters?" the guard asked politely.

"Are you really nuns?" one of the young men said, slightly slurring his words.

"Misbehave and you'll find out," LaTrelle said curtly.

"Sounds like fun," the young man said, laughing and looking around at his friends.

His friends laughed.

"Hey, c'mon buddy," the guard said.

Susan quickly grabbed the back of the young man's neck and rammed his face down on the table. Carmela applied a wristlock and forced his hand on the table. Angela pinned his shirtsleeve to the table with her knife. Marie chopped his knuckles with a ruler. The other young men were terrified and frozen.

"Ow!" the young man said, with his face flat on the table.

"Any other questions, young man?" LaTrelle asked.

"No, ma'am. No, sister. Sorry. The table is all yours," he said distortedly.

Angela pulled her knife from the table. The men scrambled away.

"Thank you. Go with God," LaTrelle called after them.

"If you sisters ever need a job, let me know," the guard said, pulling out a chair for LaTrelle. "I mean it."

LaTrelle looked over her shoulder at him and said. "Let's hope it doesn't come to that, my friend."

The guard smiled. "I'll send over a waitress."

Nappy cradled the hatbox as he and the rest of the sisters sat. They watched the crowd and the storm build over the desert to the west. A waitress soon appeared.

Without waiting for her to speak, Nappy said, "Five bottles of Evian and one Teat City Beer, please."

"Yes, sir," the waitress said and spun away.

LaTrelle looked to the other sisters. "Let's go to the Little Nuns' Room."

The nuns got up. Nappy stood up.

"You have to piss at a time like this?" he snapped.

LaTrelle smiled. "You'll be fine. Relax."

"Hurry back, *n'est-ce pas*?" he said.

After the sisters left, Nappy scanned the crowd. He slowly relaxed. He tapped to the music. He sneezed. He blew his nose. The waitress came back with their drinks. As he looked up and smiled at her, he saw something descend from the sky. He squinted at it as the waitress walked away.

"*Mon Dieu*. It's him. It has to be him. But how? Where are the nuns?" he asked quietly, desperately.

Lightning cracked in the distance and the wind began to blow.

A voice came over the PA speakers. "Everybody get inside. You can come back after the storm."

People slowly began to gather their food and drinks and headed for shelter.

Nappy looked for the nuns. He saw Julius and Eli coming closer. The thunder and lightning intensified. Lights flickered.

"Not now, Julius. Not now," Nappy lamented. "Where are the nuns?" he asked again.

Although he had it memorized, Nappy got out the prophecy from his vest and began to read it quietly aloud again.

"Beneath Heaven's Wrath, the multitude will be driven..."

Lightning cracked closer and it began to rain. Wind blew a Lost Tribes of Israel placard in front of Nappy and onto the heels and backsides of people fleeing poolside. Nappy gazed upward, and then continued to read, a bit more frantically.

"... before the Lost Tribes of Israel. *Sacre' bleu*. Nothing about *le Pape* on a flying horse."

The voice from the PA became more demanding. "Move it, people. You're sitting ducks out on the deck."

Nappy glanced down at the prophecy. "And nothing about sitting ducks," he said.

Jostling people moved more quickly from the storm.

Nappy stood on the table to look over the fleeing crowd for the nuns. He looked back to the sky.

"Where'd he go?" he wondered aloud about Julius.

With expansive wings, Eli and Julius descended through the trees and landed behind him on the pool overlook.

People stopped and gawked. A woman pointed to Eli and Julius.

"Are they real?" she asked her partner.

"This is Vegas, sweetie. Nothing's real. Let's get out of this rain," he said and ushered her forward.

Julius grabbed his bow and quiver from their scabbard and dismounted. "Stay here, Eli," he said.

Julius walked up to Nappy from behind.

"Hello, Nappy," he said threateningly.

"Julius!"

Nappy skipped around the table to put distance between the two of them. They parleyed over the wind, thunder and rain.

"The game is over," Nappy said unconvincingly. "I have the tiara."

"Then put it on," Julius challenged.

"I will, as soon as you get off," Nappy smirked.

"If you had what it takes to be a criminal, you'd have been pope long ago," Julius said dismissively.

"Go to hell!" Nappy bellowed. "I vowed on the tomb of my great-great-great-great-great grandfather to fulfill his dream, to become *le Pape*, to wear the tiara and restore our family's name to its rightful place in history."

Julius moved toward Nappy. "The tiara," he said, "and you can go in peace."

Nappy clutched the hatbox, then relaxed and smiled. Susan and Marie came up behind Julius, with cornette blowguns and darts ready. Their hair fell from the rain.

Julius' eyes followed Nappy's. He turned around to see Susan and Marie. They smiled and waved at Julius. When he looked back at Nappy, Carmela and Angela flanked the little Frenchman.

Julius said, "Really? It's come to this? Hiding behind nuns? Nappy, you have the prophecy all wrong. You're the Iconoclast, not me."

Nappy put his hands over his ears. He sneezed. "Quiet. Don't try to confuse me," he said sharply.

Julius quickly nocked an arrow and aimed his bow at Nappy. Just as quickly, the nuns aimed their blowguns at Julius.

With Nappy's heart just a few meters from the tip of his arrowhead, Julius said, "You defiled the tiara when you stole it. Then you were driven out of Rome. Flown out, technically. You are the Iconoclast."

Nappy ducked behind Carmela. He hid his face behind her hand and the blowgun. He hung onto her hand.

"You're joking!" Nappy spat. "I am the True Ruler!"

"The tiara, Nappy," Julius ordered, holding his bow and arrow steadily.

LaTrelle came up behind Julius. Her hair was down and wet. Wearing only a short silk robe, her nipples protruded through the thin material. She spoke softly into his ear, barely audible in the wind and rain.

"Julius," she said.

Julius froze. Thunder rumbled.

From behind, LaTrelle slid her hands up and on Julius' chest. "Julius," she said again.

Nappy smiled lecherously. He wiped his nose on Carmela's sleeve.

"*Mon Dieu*," he said quietly. "She looks like a goddess. Maybe *she* is the True Ruler."

Julius lowered his bow and turned to LaTrelle. They looked into each other's eyes. With her hands on his shoulders, LaTrelle tilted her head to kiss Julius. Julius leaned toward her. As their lips were about to meet, Nappy sneezed. Julius slapped the back of his neck.

"Someone just shot me with a dart," he whispered to LaTrelle and tee-tered into her.

"*Qu'est-ce?*" LaTrelle wondered.

LaTrelle turned to Nappy. Still clinging to Carmela's arm, he looked sheepish, hopeless and shrugged his shoulders.

"An accident!" he said defensively. "I sneezed into the blow gun by ac-cident."

"*Imbécile,*" she retorted.

LaTrelle could not hold Julius. He slumped to the ground and rolled on his back. LaTrelle pulled the dart from his neck and threw it at Nappy.

Livid, LaTrelle asked, "How can I get him up when I can't get him up?" She glanced at Julius' crotch. "And he was doing so well, too. Sisters, help me get him into the Forbidden Temple."

The sisters rallied around Julius, lifted him by his arms and legs and carried him head first toward the cabana. Near the entryway, a statue of Jupiter was poised to hurl a thunderbolt. Cupid aimed an arrow.

Clutching the tiara, Nappy frantically looked at the sky. Storm clouds moved toward the moon.

"Hurry!" he said. "We're losing the full moon."

He tried to follow the sisters into the cabana.

"Stay out," LaTrelle ordered.

LaTrelle gently let Julius' head go as the sisters brought him inside. She snapped the front curtain closed in Nappy's face.

Nappy slumped into a chair by the cabana. He put his two-cornered hat on the table next to him. He finally opened the hatbox and looked at the tiara. Soon, he tried to put it on. His arms quivered with effort as he forced the tiara down. Sparks sizzled between the tiara, his hands and his head.

"*Sacre' bleu!*" he cried, but somehow he held on as he continued to push.

His hair stood up, smoldered, then burst into flames. His face black-ened. Sparks from the tiara shredded his smoldering Napoleonic coat. Burns streaked his white pants.

Finally he could take no more and quickly put the tiara on the table. He grabbed a drink and doused the flames on his head. He sucked his burning fingers. He folded his arms and glared at the tiara and at the Forbidden Temple.

The sisters lay Julius on a lounge and stripped him. The putti hovered above them.

"I'll try to wake him," LaTrelle said and kissed him on the lips.

Julius did not move. LaTrelle gently slapped his face.

"The rain must have washed off the antidote," she said, "and I don't have the heart to slap him harder. We need to massage him. Hurry."

The sisters rubbed and stroked Julius' arms, thighs and manhood.

"It's working," LaTrelle said.

The sisters looked at Julius. They looked at each other. They looked back at Julius and answered in chorus.

"Mon Dieu!"

"Il est énorme!"

"Il est formidable!"

"Jésus, Marie et Joseph!"

"My wings have never beat so hard!" exclaimed the white putto.

"My wings have never been so hard!" added the red putto.

"The syzygy. Open the cabana roof," LaTrelle said urgently.

Marie and Carmela untied ropes and opened the roof. Moonlight poured in on Julius. LaTrelle looked up. Clouds neared the moon. Lightning flashed in front of it.

LaTrelle untied and opened her robe. Her breasts, torso and legs were silky smooth and firm. With robe still on, she straddled Julius.

"Keep us lined up with the moon," LaTrelle said, as she looked down at Julius.

Susan and Angela put their blowguns and darts on a coffee table, then each held one of LaTrelle's shoulders. The other sisters looked at her in awe. LaTrelle hesitated, then reached to glide Julius inside of her. Julius moaned slightly.

After somewhat recovering, Nappy tried once more to put on the tiara. Again sparks flew. With arms quivering, he got it closer, but it still would not go on. His hair stood up, steamed and smoldered. His face became more blackened; his coat more shredded. He slammed the tiara down on the table.

"Julius is not a man," he declared disgustedly.

Then, in a Napoleon-like manner, Nappy slipped his hand inside his coat and got out his cell phone. He texted "Plan B" and hit Send.

LaTrelle looked to the others. "It doesn't want to go," she said.

"Yes, it does!" the other nuns emphatically disagreed.

LaTrelle shook her head. "He may be bigger than before."

Again, the other nuns offered a chorus of encouragement.

"You can do it."

"We know you can."

"I would, if I could."

"I can't look, but I have to."

"Should I get the K-Y?"

"C'mon, Julius. Wake up! I want you to see this," said the red putto as he hovered above Julius and LaTrelle.

The white putto hovered next to him. He paged through The Kama Sutra. He showed a picture to LaTrelle.

"LaTrelle, try this position," he urged.

Bored with sitting in the rain, Nappy decided to give the tiara another try. This time, though near electrocution, he screamed orgasmically as he almost pushed the tiara onto his head.

"Yes. Yes. Oh, *Mon Dieu*, yes!"

Eli reared, whinnied and kicked.

Suddenly, powerful hands grabbed the tiara from Nappy. Damian, in tan overalls and a blue work shirt, held it away from Nappy's reaching hands.

"No!" Nappy wailed.

Inside the Forbidden Temple, the nuns looked at each other alarmed as they heard Nappy's howl.

Dressed as a policeman, Sarge broke the sanctity of the cabana. He ran in toward Angela, the closest nun. She coolly darted him. He tumbled to the floor in a heap.

Next in was Otto, running and grinning and looking about the cabana. He wore only red pants, suspenders and white tennis shoes. He carried a roll of duct tape. As soon as he spied Sister Susan he went for her, trying to tape her wrists together.

A scowling Sister Susan easily threw him. He slammed on his back onto a coffee table, shattered it, and bounced onto the floor. He rolled around in agony, with eyes squinted shut.

LaTrelle looked quickly to the sisters. "Go!" she urged.

"Julius will be pissed if he sees us here," the white putto said.

"Let's go!" hollered the red putto.

The putti flew and the nuns ran toward the cabana door. Sisters Marie and Carmela were the first to get out.

Hearing nuns run past him, Otto opened his eyes and picked up a blowgun and darts that lay under his hand on the floor. He sat up and darted Susan and Angela in the back. They crumpled outside the doorway.

Outside, Sister Marie sped past Damian and Nappy and ran along the poolside deck. She looked for the nearest exit.

Standing in a tree above the main pool, Adrian spotted her. Wearing a blue and orange Vatican Guard Speedo, he put a small vine between his teeth and swung from a large vine toward her. He swept her up on her side, carried her over a pool and let go. Both fell into the deep end of the water.

Marie fought like a panther. She attacked Adrian's eyes with her fingers and groin with her knee. She head butted his nose and, even underwater, it made his eyes water. She broke his grip. As she was about to break the surface and get a breath, Adrian pulled her back down by her leg. He rolled her over, then tied her wrists behind her back with the vine. When they came to the surface, Adrian pulled Marie to the stairs and pushed her out of the pool.

At the same time Adrian and Marie were entangled, Carmela was running in the opposite direction. Then, still hearing Nappy's screaming protests, she decided to help him. She ran back toward the cabana. Damian saw her coming and spun Nappy's two-cornered hat under her feet as Otto appeared at the doorway. Carmela slipped and fell in front of Otto, hitting her head on the unconscious heads of Sisters Susan and Angela.

Otto closed an eye, contorted his face and quickly taped the wrists of the three nuns. Then he stood, flexed his biceps over them and spit out a tooth.

"Now for a *ménage à quatre*," he drooled triumphantly over them.

LaTrelle leaned down and kissed Julius. His eyelids fluttered.

"*Au revoir, mon cheri*," she said tenderly.

LaTrelle lifted a leg and slipped off Julius. She quickly tied her robe, pulled on black silk pants, and strapped her knife to her thigh. She sliced her way out of the back of the cabana.

Outside, LaTrelle slunk through foliage to a corner of the cabana. She saw Damian squeeze Nappy's face as Nappy kept reaching for the tiara. Wind and rain shook the trees. Lightning flashed. Thunder boomed.

LaTrelle sprinted toward Damian from behind and drove a side thrust kick into his back. It knocked the air out of him with an "Oomphhhhh!" He splashed spread eagle into the pool face down. The tiara flew into the air. It fell toward Nappy's head, zapped him, then dropped in his hands. Ecstatic, he looked to LaTrelle for direction.

"Hide," she said.

"But the syzygy," he said questioningly.

"There's still time. Run," LaTrelle urged.

Nappy tucked the tiara under his arm and took off, not knowing exactly where. Lightning hit a tree. Its crown fell in a fiery heap in front of him. He stumbled, turned and ran another way.

LaTrelle planned to neutralize the guards and get back to Julius. She focused on Adrian. Adrian turned away from Sister Marie to face her. La-Trelle threw her knife. Marie bent forward and extended her hands above her back. The knife slashed the vine that tied her wrists and stuck in a palm tree.

Marie immediately threw her rosary around Adrian's neck, pulling him backwards, choking him. Adrian grabbed at the rosary with both hands. His eyes bulged as he gasped for breath. LaTrelle drove a side thrust kick into Adrian's midsection as Marie pulled away her rosary and got out of the way. Adrian slammed backwards into a palm tree, hit his head and sunk to the ground.

LaTrelle pulled her knife from the tree. She looked toward Otto and smiled. She made a slicing motion under her throat with her fingers. Otto smiled idiotically ... and ran.

LaTrelle turned to the soaking wet Sister Marie. "Let's get the other sisters," she said.

They went to the nuns who lay in front of the cabana.

Otto was running, but to where he didn't know. He'd seen enough of these nuns to last him the rest of his life. He ran like the Lion running from the Wizard in the Wizard of Oz. He was running around a statue of Pegasus, toward an exit, when he slammed into Nappy sprinting in from another direction. They smacked faces. It sounded like two watermelons hitting.

Damian was helping Adrian get up from the palm tree when they heard the collision. They looked toward the sound. Both Nappy and Otto fell backwards in opposite directions. Both hit the pool deck, knocked out. The tiara fell from Nappy's hands.

"Let's get them," Adrian said.

"But let's keep an eye out for those nuns," Damian advised, as both men jogged slowly and painfully toward Nappy and Otto.

Eli walked through the back of the torn cabana and looked down at Julius. He licked Julius' face.

Julius stirred. With eyes closed, he smiled and licked Eli.

"Mmmm, LaTrelle, the antidote," he purred. He felt his groin respond.

Eli neighed and nuzzled his muzzle into Julius' chest.

Julius blinked a few times, then pushed himself up and looked around. Eli backed away. Through the cabana door, Julius saw LaTrelle and Marie cut the other nuns loose from Otto's duct tape and revive them.

"Jesus, they're like a Hydra," he mumbled.

Eli neighed and nodded his head.

Julius looked down at himself. "Wonder what I've been doing."

He got up, stepped over the unconscious Sarge, and pulled on his pants and unbuttoned shirt.

"Wonder what Sarge has been doing," he said as he dressed.

Then he saw LaTrelle watching him through the cabana door.

LaTrelle turned to Marie and Carmela, who were helping Susan and Angela stand.

"Get them out of here," she told them.

"But le Pape," Marie protested, looking at the cabana.

Julius stood in its doorway. Eli's head appeared over Julius' shoulder.

"I'll take care of him," LaTrelle said, looking at Julius. "We have unfinished business."

Julius smiled. "There's nothing scarier than a nun with a vendetta," he conceded.

LaTrelle faced him squarely. The other nuns looked on.

"I became a nun to stay close to you. I stayed a nun to get even," she said.

"That's why you stole the tiara?" Julius asked incredulously.

"That's nothing compared to what you took from me," LaTrelle argued hotly.

Julius resigned himself to the confrontation.

"Then let's settle this," he said. "You can't keep beating up my men."

"What do you suggest?" LaTrelle asked.

Julius smiled. "When in Vegas, do as the Vegans do," he said.

"I don't know what that is. This is my first time here," LaTrelle confessed.

"Then trust me," Julius said kindly.

"Ha! Never again," LaTrelle retorted.

"I had to be about my father's business," Julius explained.

"Your father was *le Pape,* not God," LaTrelle argued.

"Not in his mind," Julius said.

Damian and Adrian had roused Nappy and Otto. Damian had a sullen Nappy by his collar and pushed him forward. Nappy's face, hands, hair and pants were singed. His coat tattered. He and Otto had huge red welts on their foreheads, bruised noses and fat, bloody lips.

Adrian carried the tiara. Otto walked next to him. The four men walked up to the Forbidden Temple. Otto spat out a tooth.

"The tiara, Your Holiness," Adrian said, holding up the prize.

Julius lovingly looked at the tiara with teary eyes. "Julius II's tiara," he said to Adrian. "Thank you."

Adrian offered the crown to Julius. Julius reached for it, then pulled back.

Nappy squirmed towards it, fighting Damian's grip.

"It's mine!" Nappy squealed.

Damian rapped Nappy in the head. "Shut up." To Julius, he said, "It's yours, Your Holiness. Take it."

Julius shook his head slightly. "Not yet," he said.

"Give it to me!" Nappy demanded.

Damian smacked him again.

"Enough!" LaTrelle said. "How would the Vegans settle this?" she asked Julius.

"At the tables," he said simply.

Suddenly a voice from the PA blared. "Folks, the storm is over. You can go outside now."

Rowdy people in swimwear and robes and drinks in hand immediately filled the pool area. Some mingled around. Some jumped in the water. Basilica staff worked the bars and tables. Soon, a few people trickled toward the Forbidden Temple. When they saw Julius, LaTrelle, the nuns, a winged horse, Nappy and the other men, they stopped. Some smiled, others look confused.

Sarge staggered out of the cabana toward his friends. Suddenly, he slapped his neck and fell onto the pavement. A dart stuck in his neck.

Angela lowered her blowgun and smiled. The nuns looked at her.

"I couldn't help myself," she shrugged.

The trickle became a torrent as people crowded around the Forbidden Temple. A murmur spread through the crowd as some recognized Julius.

"That's the pope."

"Here?"

"That's Pope Julius."

"It can't be."

"I'm sure it is."

"I thought he was dead."

"He doesn't look it."

Julius craned his neck and looked into the crowd.

"We need a dealer," he said.

A young woman walked out of the crowd. She wore a visor, black pants, black shoes, a white long-sleeve shirt with sleeves held in place with bright red sleeve garters. She smiled and bowed deferentially.

"I can help you, Your Holiness. I'm Terri, the pit boss. What's your game?" she asked.

"Blackjack."

146

"This way," she said.

Terri walked toward a Blackjack table under a lit canopy. A crowd followed.

Julius turned to LaTrelle and said. "We'll play a few practice hands so you get the hang of the game."

"No need," she confided. "After you left ..."

Nappy laughed maniacally, "... she was a dealer at Casino de Monte-Carlo. Julius, you're a fool."

Terri removed the weather cover from the table. She looked at Julius and asked, "The stakes?"

Julius took the tiara from Adrian. He put it in the betting area. It sparkled under the lights.

The crowd collectively exclaimed, "Ooooo. Ahhhhh. Wow! Holy shit! Look at that. Whoa."

"That'd look great with this jumpsuit," the Elvis Impersonator declared.

Nappy frothed at the mouth. His eyes bulged. He reached for the tiara. Damian pulled him back by the collar.

"I can't cover that," Terri said.

"We won't play against you, only against each other. One hand, winner take all," Julius said.

"Got it. Who are the players?" Terri asked.

LaTrelle took a center seat at the table. Julius sat on LaTrelle's right. Damian pushed Nappy onto a chair on LaTrelle's left.

"The three of us," Julius said.

Julius looked to LaTrelle and Nappy. "Here's your chance to get even, LaTrelle. If either of you win, I'll break my vow of celibacy and the tiara is yours."

Nappy leaned forward and asked LaTrelle, "Will you still take him?"

"Oui ... to keep the convent open," she explained.

Julius tipped back in his chair and looked at the partly cloudy sky. The full moon shone in his eyes. He removed his ring and put it in the side bet area.

"And I'll throw in the papal ring," Julius said.

The crowd let out a long, soft sigh.

"I'd play for that," the Liberace Impersonator said with a slick smile.

Nappy leaned forward to look at LaTrelle again. "If you win, I win, *n'est-ce pas?*" he asked.

Julius addressed Terri. "We'll play by the basic rules. No splits."

Terri shuffled, then dealt Julius the first card. "Seven of diamonds," she called.

Terri turned over and tossed LaTrelle's first card. "Jack of hearts," she said.

Terri dealt Nappy his first card. "Three of hearts," she called.

Nappy whimpered and shuddered. He squeezed his knees together as if he was about to piss in his pants.

Terri dealt Julius his second card. "Four of spades. Makes eleven."

LaTrelle got her second card.

"Four of clubs. For fourteen," Terri said.

Nappy squirmed on his hands.

"Eight of diamonds. Makes eleven," Terri announced.

Nappy bit his fist.

Julius tapped the table.

Terri tossed him another card. "Eight of hearts, for nineteen."

LaTrelle waved for another card.

Terri dealt her a six of hearts. "Good for twenty," Terri said.

LaTrelle looked at Nappy. Nappy tapped the table.

"Nine of clubs," Terri announced as the card hit the table. "Good for twenty."

Nappy joyously threw his hands in the air.

"*Incroyable!*" he cried.

Nappy turned to LaTrelle and happily said, "I win, you win."

Terri turned to Julius. He tapped the table. She dealt.

"Five of diamonds. Busted," Terri said.

The crowd gasped and murmured. The men of the Fellowship of the Tiara looked at one another.

Julius shrugged and said, "*Que sera sera.*"

Nappy jumped out of his chair and danced. "We win! I am everything!" he screamed joyously, looking up and spinning around in a circle with his arms raised.

LaTrelle tapped the table. Terri flipped a card.

Nappy put his hands on the table and glared at LaTrelle.

"What are you doing?" he demanded.

"Ace of clubs. Twenty-one," Terri proclaimed.

The crowd celebrated.

"Yea!"

"Woo-hoo!"

"You go, Sista!"

Julius smiled at her. "Well played."

"You win, I win?" Nappy asked uncertainly.

"With the tiara I can keep the convent open without you," LaTrelle said simply.

Nappy slammed his fists on the table, and then looked at Terri. "Hit me!" he raved.

As Terri dealt Nappy's last card, a strong wind and roar struck the players. Trees swayed. Cards flew off the table. Everyone looked up. A blinding white light shone down.

With everyone distracted, Nappy grabbed the tiara and ran. His helicopter was overhead. It unfurled a rope ladder. Nappy snagged it with one hand and held the tiara with the other. The helicopter hovered above the trees and lifted Nappy off the ground. He began to climb the ladder.

Shielding her eyes from the light, LaTrelle saw Nappy, hurdled the Blackjack table and went after him. She caught the last rung of the ladder. She swung as if hanging from a trapeze and dangled just below Nappy.

Julius had sprinted from his chair, pocketed the papal ring and just missed grabbing the ladder's bottom rung.

LaTrelle looked down at him as the helicopter lifted her and Nappy.

"*Que sera sera!*" she hollered.

"I don't think so!" he hollered back as he looked at her. Then he turned toward the cabana and whistled.

Eli pinned his ears back and galloped from the cabana toward Julius. Julius jumped on Eli's back and urged him upward toward the helicopter. Eli spread his wings and took off.

People poolside looked up and stared.

"This is better than Cirque du Soleil," one of them said.

Astride Eli and above The Basilica pools, Julius took his bow and nocked an arrow.

Nappy looked down at LaTrelle. LaTrelle looked up at Nappy as she pulled herself up a few rungs. Her legs swung freely. He stepped on her hands.

"Now whose side are you on, Sister?" he chided. Then he caught sight of Julius. "Oh, *fils de pute!*" he squealed, as he saw Julius release an arrow.

The rope ladder tilted.

"Aaaaaaaaaiiiiiiii!" Nappy screamed.

Nappy looked up. One side of the ladder was cut. He forced himself to climb higher. A few more steps and he'd be inside the helicopter.

LaTrelle looked down at Julius. Julius shot again. The arrow severed the ladder. The ladder, LaTrelle, Nappy and the tiara fell. Julius quickly plucked LaTrelle out of the air before she fell too far and pulled her astride Eli. They watched Nappy splash into the deep end of the large pool and disappear, as the tiara floated down like a parachute. It landed on the head of the Elvis Impersonator.

LaTrelle looked over her shoulder at Julius and smiled. As they were about to kiss, Eli turned hard. The helicopter had come back for them. It almost knocked them out of the air, then flew over The Basilica and was gone. LaTrelle patted Eli and leaned forward near his ear.

"Thank you, Flying Horse," she said affectionately.

Adrian had dove into the pool and surfaced with a charred and nearly drowned Nappy. He brought him to the poolside steps. Damian and Otto dragged Nappy out and laid him on the pavement near a statue of Neptune holding a trident.

Eli, Julius and LaTrelle landed by them. The Elvis Impersonator walked up to Julius.

"This belongs to you, Your Holiness," he said as he removed the tiara from his head. "I'm already The King. I don't need to be Pope." He handed the tiara to Julius.

"Thank you," Julius said appreciatively. "Thank you very much."

Eyes enraged, Nappy spit up and coughed up water. Damian held him back as he struggled to get to the tiara.

"Mine. Mine. It belongs to me!" he shrieked.

With the tiara in hand, Julius swung off of Eli.

"It's over, Nappy," he pronounced.

Nappy pointed a shaking finger to Elvis.

"How can he wear it, but not me?" he bellowed.

"Elvis is the True Ruler," Julius explained simply.

"He's an imposter," Nappy scoffed.

"Oh no," Julius corrected. "He personifies a higher power, as do I."

"No!" Nappy raved.

Julius smiled as he asked, "Want to try it again?"

Without waiting for an answer, Julius offered Nappy the tiara. Nappy grabbed it with both hands and tried to quickly shove it on his head. Zapped harder than ever, Nappy slammed to the pavement hard on his butt. The tiara rolled from his hands. His eyes rolled to the top of his head. His clothes and body steamed. He shook his head, then looked at Julius, eyes wide and wild.

Damian bent down for the tiara. Nappy sprawled forward on his stomach and beat him to it, grabbing it with one hand. As Damian went to take it from him, Julius touched Damian's arm. Nappy defiantly clutched the tiara to his chest.

"Let him have it," Julius said. "We need to fulfill the prophecy. You know what to do," he added and nodded to Damian.

Damian grabbed one of Nappy's hands, pulled it away from the tiara, and put a wristlock on him, torquing his wrist in ways it was not meant to go. Nappy immediately screamed in pain.

"Ow! *Jésus!* Take it. It's yours. Let me go!" He begged.

Damian held the wristlock on him. Nappy dropped the tiara. Otto snatched it up.

Julius stood over Nappy and asked, "Do you promise to never try to steal the tiara again, in any way, shape or form?"

"*Oui!*"

"And you renounce all vows to the papacy forever?" Julius asked.

Nappy stayed silent. Julius nodded at Damian to increase the pain.

"Ow! Ow! Ow! *Oui.* I will never again attempt to become *le Pape!*" he shrieked.

"And you promise to never invade Russia …" Julius continued.

Nappy squirmed and squealed. "Ow! *Oui.* Never," he promised.

"And reimburse the Vatican for our travel expenses, plus the loss of the Lear," Julius added.

Nappy nodded. "Of course, your expenses."

"Oh, one more thing …" Julius said as an after thought.

"*Mon Dieu.* What?" Nappy asked incredulously.

"Is the room your great-great-great-great-great grandfather used to imprison Pius VII still functional?" Julius asked.

"*Oui.* I planned to keep you there after crowning myself *le Pape,*" Nappy said.

"You will make it available to the Vatican," Julius said firmly.

Nappy hesitated. Damian twisted Nappy's wrist.

"Ow! Agreed. *D'accord,*" the little man said.

"Let him go, Damian," Julius said, blessing Nappy with a sign of the cross. "The Iconoclast's vow has been broken."

Damian let Nappy go.

Nappy dropped his head. "I was so close," he wept softly, "so close to everything."

Sarge staggered over to the group. Sister Angela aimed her blowgun at him, but Susan lowered Angela's arm. Angela shrugged.

LaTrelle slipped off Eli and went to Julius. They stood heart to heart and looked into each other's eyes.

"It's over," Julius said softly.

"I know. I won the tiara," LaTrelle said.

"No. Nappy never got his last card," Julius countered.

"He couldn't beat me, only tie me," LaTrelle said.

"I can tie you, too," Julius said with a smile.

"Like before?" LaTrelle asked hopefully.

"Better than before. I know more knots now."

LaTrelle put her hands on Julius' chest. "That would make us even, but you're still *le Pape*," she said.

"No problem. Religion means to tie. I'd be fulfilling my duty if I tie you up," Julius reasoned.

"Hmmmmmm, so you tie me up and I have a religious experience?"

"*Oui.* I win, you win," Julius agreed.

LaTrelle nodded toward Nappy. "Then what do you plan to do to him?"

"Nothing, if he keeps his promises to stop stealing, conquering and trying to become pope," Julius answered.

"So, the sisters and I are out of work," LaTrelle concluded and dropped her hands from Julius' chest.

"There's work for you at the Vatican," said a voice.

St. Peter walked through the crowd. He wore an admiral uniform. The Fellowship of the Tiara and the nuns gathered around him.

"Who are you to make such an offer?" LaTrelle asked curiously.

"He's St. Peter, himself, LaTrelle," Julius said with a smile.

"Le gatekeeper of heaven?" she asked, wanting to believe.

"In the flesh, as flesh as I can be at the moment, anyway," Peter confirmed. Then he spoke to Julius. "You figured out the prophecy."

"So it seems," Julius said.

"Thank God," Peter said emphatically. "I got all confused with the syzygy, the Trinity and a *ménage à trois*."

"Nothing a *ménage à quatre* couldn't fix," Otto said.

Julius addressed Peter. "Nappy was confused, too. It seems he thought the syzygy and Trinity were the same thing."

"They aren't?" a surprised Peter asked.

"Nope," Julius answered.

"That went right over my head," Peter said.

"LaTrelle, Nappy and I were the Trinity," Julius explained. "The prophecy states Heaven's Crown would be exchanged through the hands of the Trinity. What better way to do that than deal each of us a hand of Blackjack and play for the tiara?"

"That makes sense," Peter acknowledged, then paused for a moment and asked, "How'd you know Nappy was the Iconoclast?"

"I didn't until a few minutes ago when Nappy said he vowed to become pope on the tomb of his great-great-great-great-great grandfather. I realized then the prophecy referred to his vow and his theft of the tiara."

"Brilliant!" Peter exclaimed. "And the True Ruler?"

"That part always confused me until I saw The King. Then it was simply a matter of getting the tiara to fall from the heavens to him," Julius said simply.

"And reconcile secular with spiritual," LaTrelle concluded.

"As above so below," Peter added.

"Speaking of which, were you crucified upside down or not?" Julius asked.

Peter's eyes twinkled as he said, "It depends on your point of view."

Julius resigned himself to Peter's answer, but said, "We still don't see eye to eye."

Julius turned to LaTrelle. "What do you think of the job offer?" he asked.

"*Vraiment?*" she asked. "My sisters and I can live and work at the Vatican?"

"With all the kielbasa you can eat," Julius assured her.

"Sisters, what do you think?" LaTrelle asked.

The sisters answered in unison, saying, "*Oui. Mais oui. Bien sûr. D'accord.*"

"Great!" Julius said. "The Vatican needs its own parkour team."

No one in the crowd comprehended everything that had gone on, but everyone was happy, except Nappy.

Jason and the Lost Tribes of Israel arrived poolside and began to set up. Patti retrieved the band's placard that blew over in the wind. Excitedly, she pointed to Julius.

"It's Father Pope Holiest!" she squealed.

Jason appraised the guards, St. Peter, Nappy and the nuns. He smacked his head.

"And the Village People!" he exclaimed. "We're opening for the Village People!"

Soon, the band started to play. The Elvis Impersonator sang with them. People danced. Julius' men danced with the nuns. Julius danced with La-Trelle. St. Peter danced with the Liberace Impersonator.

Epilogue

AS NEWS OF Pope Julius' whereabouts became public, reporters swarmed to Las Vegas. For days, headlines captured the Fellowship of the Tiara's story.

Day 1 Headlines:
> *Julius V Alive and Well in Vegas*
> *Pope's Horse Rolls Craps; Takes Out Cuban MiG*

There was a prominent photo of Otto and Sister Susan holding a Cuban flag in front of Eli. The others posed with them.

Day 2 Headline:
> *Pope & Entourage Win Big in Vegas for Poor*

One photo showed Julius and the others holding massive amounts of coin from slot machine jackpots.

Day 3 Headlines:
> *Julius V Wins High Stakes Celebrity Poker*
> *Every Cent to Charity*

Photos of Julius and LaTrelle with cigars and stacks of chips on a poker table in front of them went viral.

Day 4 Headlines:

Pope Says High Mass at Basilica – Hottest Show in Vegas

Vegas Resorts Commit to Weekly Tithe for Poor

Photos showed a massive crowd in attendance at Mass at The Basilica.

Sitting in his office, Cardinal Richelieu read the Vatican newspaper, heralding the triumphs of the triumphant Pope Julius. He crumpled the newspaper in disgust.

"Like a cat, he lands on his feet," Richelieu lamented.

"He's become a serious pope," Monsignor Tupelli observed.

"He's a freak," Richelieu corrected. "Let's steal the tiara!" he suggested excitedly.

Tupelli responded as he often did. "Let me think about it," he said.

An airliner landed at Leonardo da Vinci Airport in Rome. The Fellowship of the Tiara and the sisters deplaned. Thousands of cheering people greeted them.

Beginning that day and for the next several months, headlines throughout the world announced Vatican news as never before.

Pope Safely Returns to Vatican

Missions Impossible: Pope Recovers Tiara ~ Redeems Las Vegas

One month later

Pope Supports Sex Education

Julius says, "Our priests have a lot to learn."

Two months later

Catholic Church OKs Birth Control

Pope says, "Biblical mission accomplished. The earth's been populated."

Two and a half months later

Catholic Church Recants – Masturbation Not a Sin

Pope says, "Idle hands are the devil's workshop."

Three months later

Pope Wins Horseback Archery World Title

Huns Promise Not to Invade Rome

Three and a half months later

Sisters de Jeanne d'Arc Win World Parkour Team Title

Sister LaTrelle Takes Individual Title

Five months later

Catholic Priests and Nuns Can Marry

Pope proclaims, "Celibacy is an option, not a command."

Six months later

Catholic Church – Women Allowed to Become Priests

Pope asks "Why not?"

Six and a half months later

Catholic Church – Men Allowed to Become Nuns

Pope says, "It's the right thing to do."

Seven months later

Cardinal Plots to Steal Tiara of Julius II

Pope says, "It's the wrong thing to do."

Disgraced Cardinal "Retired" to French Villa

Inside Le Palais Des Papes, Nappy unlocked the room where Napoleon imprisoned Pope Pius VII, and ushered in the frail Cardinal Richelieu. The cardinal stumbled. Nappy caught him and eased him onto a chair. The teary-eyed cardinal touched Nappy on the arm.

"Thank you, my son," the cardinal said appreciatively. "I could not expect better treatment from your great-great-great-great-great grandfather."

"No, you couldn't," Nappy agreed. "But please, call him Napoleon."

Seven and a half months later

Sister LaTrelle says, "Yes!"

Pope says, "She actually said 'Oui!'"

On the morning of his wedding day, Julius served breakfast to Rome's poor in a church basement. Men came by in line with their meal trays.

"Congratulations to you, Your Holiness, and Sister LaTrelle," a bald old man said as Julius scooped eggs and sausage onto his plate. "We think your marriage is great."

Julius smiled. "Thank you. So do I."

In a confidential tone, the man added, "You know, celibacy never made me holier, just hornier."

An old man with a walker was behind him in line.

"Yep. Enjoy yourself while you can," he advised Julius. "Look at us. You'll be celibate again soon enough, when you're old enough."

"And for long enough," the first man added. "We can't even wank now."

"Too bad," Julius empathized. "It's not a sin anymore."

Later that morning, a sweaty Julius worked at the blacksmith forge inside the Papal Smithy. The steel brace was orange hot as he pounded, bent and tempered it in a water bath. When done, he removed his earplugs.

The white putto's wings beat merrily as he said, "Julius, you have company."

The red putto flapped next to the white one and admonished, "Don't spoil the surprise."

159

Julius smiled at the putti as he heard footsteps. "The surprise is for La-Trelle, not these guys."

Four workmen came down the stairs and into the smithy.

"We're here for the carriage, Your Holiness," the foreman said.

"Hi, Stefan," Julius said. He pointed to a stack of metal pieces. "Those pieces are still hot, so take them last. Here are the assembly instructions."

Julius handed Stefan a sheet of paper.

"We'll take care of it," Stefan said.

"Thank you."

That afternoon, music played softly in the Vatican Gardens. Four hundred wedding guests sat in chairs on the lawn, awaiting the bride. Guests included Julius II Games competitors, the old Amish couple, Gino, Alfonso, the witches, the kidnapped priest, apostles, some of Nappy's soldiers, plus Buddhists, Greek Orthodox and Roman Catholic clergy, imams, shamans, Elvis and other celebrities, royalty, heads of state and the two old men to whom Julius served breakfast. Thousands more watched on monitors in St. Peter's Square and a billion throughout the world. The atmosphere was electric.

Terri, The Basilica's pit boss, read her program. She nudged the Liberace Impersonator next to her.

"It says here the Officiate is St. Peter," Terri said.

The Liberace Impersonator smiled widely and said, "I'll save the last dance for him."

St. Peter and Julius stood at the head of the wedding aisle. The bridesmaids were Angela, Susan, Marie and Carmela. They were paired with Sarge, Otto, Adrian and Damian. The bridesmaids wore champagne colored dresses; the men wore dark brown tuxedos, except Otto. He trashed his the night before at the bachelors' party. He wore a sleeveless T-shirt tuxedo with a pink bow tie, brown pants with a pink stripe up each leg, and suspenders.

The piano player began to play, "Here Comes the Bride". The guests stood. LaTrelle, in a flowing white wedding gown, walked proudly up the aisle with her elderly father. He wore a black tux. When she reached Julius, she smiled at him and bowed lightly to St. Peter. They smiled back.

"You always did look good in a little white dress," Julius said to La-Trelle.

In bed with an almost naked Milk and Cookie in a Basilica Resort suite, Nappy watched the wedding on TV. Cookie wore his unbuttoned Napoleonic coat. Milk had on his two-cornered hat.

"Let's do it again, Sweetie," Milk cooed as she nuzzled him.

"Just a minute," Nappy said, slightly irritated. "I want to see this."

"I want to see this!" Cookie teased and lifted the sheet, peeking at Nappy. Nappy whipped the sheet out of her hand. "Not until *le Pape* is married," he snapped.

Back in the Vatican Gardens, Julius and LaTrelle expressed the most simple, most loving of vows. "You win, I win," they said together to each other.

After they exchanged rings, Peter said, "Julius and LaTrelle, I pronounce you *Le Pape* and wife. You may kiss."

They did.

Television cameras captured the world's reactions. There were cheers from monasteries, convents, castles, stadiums, bars, prisons, churches, offices and airports, to armies, bush people, Village People, astronauts and school children. Everyone was ecstatic.

Cardinal Richelieu watched the wedding ceremony on the television in his apartment. He strained forward in his chair.

"*Mon Dieu.* LaTrelle is gorgeous. Maybe Julius is a serious pope," he said to himself.

At the wedding announcers ' table in the Vatican Gardens, off to the side where Julius and LaTrelle stood waving to guests, PAGAN television announcers , Neil and Lisa, gave commentary.

"There you have it, folks," Neil said. "Pope Julius V is no longer the world's most eligible bachelor."

Lisa beamed radiantly. "This wedding is one of the most important the world has ever seen," she said.

"Public opinion is solidly in favor of it," Neil added.

"People love the Papal Couple," Lisa concluded.

Beneath the dome of St. Peter's Basilica, guests ambled about the Vatican Gardens, replete with Vegas-like fountains and pathways. Inside the Vatican Dining Hall, the wedding party hosted a receiving line. Food and drink and jocularity flowed.

Later, Peter stood at the head table, with Julius and LaTrelle seated by him. He rapped his glass with a knife. The room slowly quieted.

"Friends," Peter began, "waiters are bringing champagne. Please join us for a toast to the bride and groom. Father Tupelli, can you clear some of these tables?" Peter asked with a sweep of his hand.

The demoted Tupelli bussed tables with a dour look on his face. As he carried a heavy tray of dishes, he tripped and fell into the champagne cart. The cart tipped on its side. Champagne, glasses and plates crashed to the floor.

Peter turned to Julius and mumbled, "I told you to lock him up with Richelieu."

Julius smiled at Peter. "Maybe I should. The champagne was a present from Nappy." Then Julius spoke into the mic. "Is there a messiah in the house? We need more champagne."

The crowd laughed. Julius' mother, Sister Lorraine, got up from her chair and went to a pretty, young, dark-haired woman seated at a table near the head table.

"Christina," she implored, "they have no champagne."

"What would you have me do?" Christina asked. "My hour has not yet come."

Lorraine motioned two waiters over. "Do whatever she tells you," she said, nodding toward Christina. Then she went back to her seat.

Christina sat thoughtfully for a moment, looking at the overturned champagne cart. Tupelli picked up dishes. The guests began to talk to one another again.

After a moment, Christina turned to the waiters and said, "Fill some empty wine boxes full of water, then draw a glass for Peter."

They removed the bladder from the boxes, filled the bladders with water and put them back in place. A waiter put a box on the table and poured Peter a glass. It bubbled delightfully.

"Box champagne?" Peter said to the waiter, amused. He took a sip. He was stunned. He took another. "Where did you get this?" he asked incredulously.

"It was water just a second ago. She told us to do it," the waiter said, pointing to Christina, who sat nearby.

Peter looked at Christina and smiled. "I'll be damned," he said. "This is godamazing! I haven't had anything like this since the Last Supper. Pass it around."

After waiters filled the guests' glasses, Peter rapped a box of champagne, to no effect, then rapped a glass. The hall quieted.

"Let's try again," Peter said. "Folks, we never know what may be the catalyst for love. It could be alcohol, a crucifixion, a song or a walk in the park. But for our lucky couple, Julius and LaTrelle, it was theft, pure and simple. I'm not talking about the tiara, although Julius told me he let La-Trelle get away with it – twice."

LaTrelle playfully glared at Julius.

"I'm talking about how they stole each other's heart in an unforgiveable act of unbelievable passion of biblical proportion. But can you give something that's been stolen from you; and can you steal something that's been given freely? For fun, let's say you can. Now their reward for that theft is

Life, not life in prison, at least let's hope that's not what their marriage turns into, but a lifetime together. May it be joyous, long and fulfilling."

"And may the sun never set on the Catholic Empire!" the tipsy red putto bellowed unnoticed at Julius' shoulder.

He clinked glasses with the white putto. They drank, and then both crashed face down on the table.

Glasses were raised and emptied. Music played. The reception continued as:

Jason and the Lost Tribes of Israel played and Elvis sang.

Julius and LaTrelle danced the first dance.

Sister Susan caught LaTrelle's bouquet.

Julius took off LaTrelle's garter and tossed it. Otto jumped up, grabbed it out of the air and wore it around his neck. Sister Susan clapped and planted a big , happy kiss on Otto, then sat down and let him slip the garter on her leg. When he had erotically delivered it up her thigh, Otto did a celebratory robot dance.

After mingling among guests, Lorraine sat between the Cuban MiG pilots, who were dressed in their flight suits. As the pilots told their story of shooting down the papal Lear, one made machine gun motions with his hands. The other motioned a plane going down. The three laughed riotously.

Finally, St. Peter again took the microphone. When the crowded quieted, he said, "Ladies and gentlemen, I'd like to present the bride and groom with a special gift. Bring Eli in, please."

Eli drew the wedding carriage Julius built to the head table. It looked like an Amish buggy. It was adorned with brown and champagne colored streamers. The canopy was down.

"That's beautiful," LaTrelle said to Julius.

"LaTrelle, Julius, maybe you can make that syzygy after all," Peter said with a smile.

In a flash of light, Eli got his wings back. People gasped.

"How did he do that?" a befuddled Bella asked.

"That's real magic!" Stella squealed.

Julius and LaTrelle went to Eli and the carriage. Julius gave LaTrelle a hand up, then got in and took the reins.

They looked to the crowd and said, "Thanks, everyone. Love to you all."

To cheers from the guests, Eli lifted off. The hall doors opened as he flew slowly towards them. Julius and LaTrelle waved. Julius flashed the peace sign. He and LaTrelle kissed and they disappeared into the night.

Eli took Julius and LaTrelle over the Vatican, Rome and the full moon-lit Mediterranean. The carriage's orange slow-moving vehicle triangle disappeared into the night.

Glossary – French to English, unless otherwise specified

au revoir – goodbye

bien sûr – of course

bonjour – good day

bras d'honneur – the French equivalent to "the finger," performed by slapping one's bicep with one hand, while making a fist and raising it with the other.

coitus interruptus – to interrupt sexual intercourse

d'accord – agreed

fils de pute – son of a bitch

il est énorme – it is enormous

il est formidable – it is formidable

imbécile – imbecile

impossible – impossible

incroyable – incredible

jawohl – yes [German]

Jésus, Marie et Joseph – Jesus, Mary and Joseph

Le Palais des Papes – The Palace of the Popes

le Pape – the Pope, usually refers to Julius

mais – but

Mon Dieu – My God

Mein Gott – My God [German}

ménage à quatre – a sexual foursome

ménage à trois – a sexual threesome

mon père – my father

que sera sera – what will be, will be

Sacré bleu – a French curse

oui – yes

About the Author

BORN IN CHICAGO and raised in Kansas, Steve Francis struggled to get away from it all ever since he could crawl. After "earning" two college degrees and floundering in the related jobs they helped him to hate, he made his way to the West Coast. In Oregon, he connected with Jack Schwarz, who was, at the time, considered to be one of the most gifted and influential teachers of mind-body controls and intuitive skills in the world. [Jack was the subject of many studies conducted by major research centers around the world. In the U.S. those included The Menninger Foundation's Psychophysiology Laboratory, The Stanford Research Institute and Langley-Porter. So, Jack was the psychic and Steve was the sidekick.]

Steve worked and studied with Jack for several years and the two collaborated on one of Jack's later books, "It's Not What You Eat, But What Eats You." During that time, Steve was also a yoga instructor, a bartender and co-owner of a martial arts studio that featured full-contact kick boxing. Although certain he didn't get hit in the head that often, Steve made several major questionable decisions. So, in 1989, he abandoned Oregon, came to Montana and that has been home ever since.

Steve has been fortunate enough to balance his Catholic upbringing not only with work with Jack Schwarz, George Leonard and other teachers, but also with several Lakota and Blackfeet families who welcome him to their ceremonies. He also teaches critical thinking and writing at Montana State University. In addition, he gives talks on the Hero's Journey and how important both comedy and drama are to it. These eclectic experiences give the impetus needed to create the prophetic action and characters he hopes you will enjoy in Julius V~Warrior Pope. A sequel is in the works.

Like us on Facebook at https://www.facebook.com/JuliusV.WarriorPope.
Check out Steve's other work and blog at www.consciousevolution.info.